Buffalo Dope

A Novel

by

Joseph Sigurdson

Buffalo Dope

Copyright © 2021 Joseph Sigurdson

All rights reserved.

No part of this publication may be reproduced, distributed, or transmitted in any form or by any means, including photocopying, recording, or other electronic or mechanical methods, without the prior written permission of the publisher, except in brief quotations embodied in critical reviews, citations, and literary journals for noncommercial uses permitted by copyright law.

This is a work of fiction. Names, characters, businesses, places, events, locales, and incidents are either the products of the author's imagination or used in a fictitious manner. Any resemblance to actual persons, living or dead, or actual events is purely coincidental.

ISBN-13: 978-0-578-99873-2

Cover design by Matthew Revert

Printed in the U.S.A.

For more titles and inquiries, please visit:

www.thirtywestph.com

For the punks I grew up with.

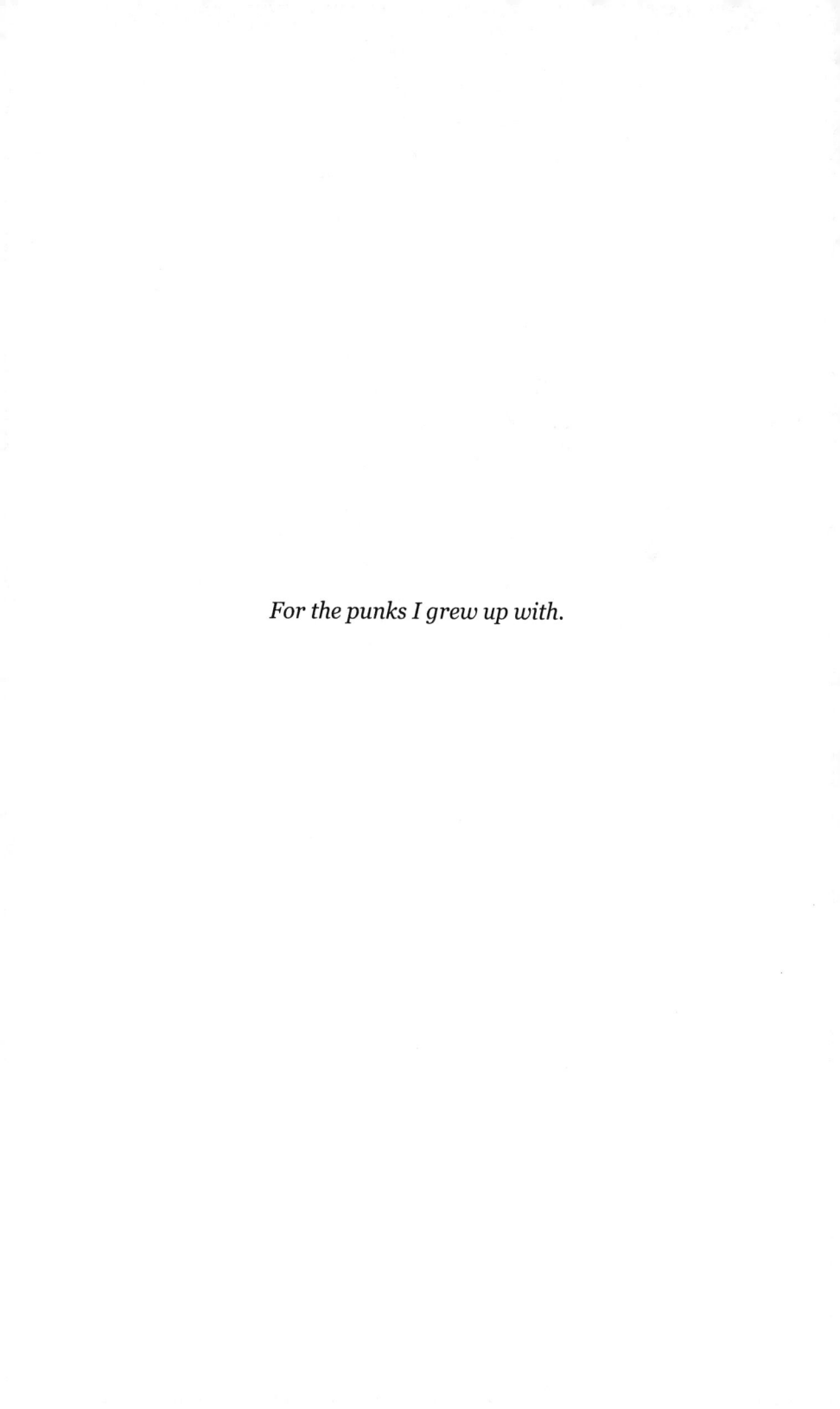

Buffalo Dope

I.

So I was all like, "Ma, the fuckin' bathtub's cavin' in!" I bet you she heard me. We'd been having problems in the bathroom for a while. Piping issues. Shit like that. First there came a slow drip from the lines below the sink. I found the spot and wrapped it in a pound of duct tape. Then the toilet started smelling like a fuckin' sewer, no matter how many times we cleaned it. The issue must've been deeper. Some disturbance in the guts of the house that was burping its way up through the toilet. It came and went—the smell. But now, the bathtub was sunken pretty deep. Bear in mind, this thing was on the second floor, so it was dropping, like, sixteen feet onto the living room table if it fell through.

"It's all fucked up, Ma!"

She didn't respond, wherever she was.

I had places to be, so I stripped naked, minus the gold crucifix around my neck. Goosebumps were scattered across my whole body. My feet were frozen to the tile floor. In Buffalo's winter, it doesn't matter how high you blast the heat—the bathroom's still gonna be ice cold. I hit the handle, made it spit, then rain, adjusted it as so, and impatiently waited for it to heat up. It always took forever. Our antique sewer piping probably wasn't much help.

When it was finally ready, I slowly lifted one leg into the shower. I put some weight into it, then progressively applied more, all the while keeping one leg on the outside in case the whole fuckin' thing fell through.

I had most of my weight pushed in, and it wasn't budging, so I figured it'd be safe. Maybe the foundation was still intact. I don't know. Is that the terminology? I know nothing of carpentry. A lot of dudes have a dad to teach them that, but my dad was in prison for life for murdering someone. Yeah. And Ma sure as shit wasn't much of a parent. She didn't even make my lunch for me in kindergarten. I used to pretend to be surprised or disappointed when I opened my bag, just to be like the other kids. I'd say, "Aw, yes! Fruit snacks!" But I already knew the fruit snacks were there because I put them there. That's just a funny example. I'm not genuinely bitching about that. She drinks, among other things.

So, I showered until my back was ash. In a cold climate, it was hard not to cherish such great warmth. Apparently, I pushed the limit a little too far, though, because the shower went *crink!* and fell even more into the floor. I stood there motionless, eyes wide, asshole puckered. I waited a few moments, then ever so slowly, pulled the curtain away, and stepped out.

The tile beside the tub was now all jagged and protruding upright.

"Ma!"

Silence.

◆◆◆

I got all bundled up but was still cold when I stepped out into the snow. I never shoveled the driveway. Too much work. If I did, I just made two thin paths for my car's tires. I had a rusty Nissan Sentra named Sheila. Twelve years old. Well over one-hundred thousand miles on that little thing. I had no clue how she still worked, but she did. I didn't even have snow tires.

That morning, Sheila was encrusted with shiny slabs of ice, just like every other winter morning in fuckin' Buffalo, New York. The Queen City. The City of Good Neighbors. The Arctic tundra, basically. Why humans ever settled there in the first place is beyond me. I dinged the locks and ripped the back door open from its icy hold. A breath of snow came down from the roof and fell into the back seat. That always happened. I took the back end of the snowbrush and started digging it into the ice on the windshield. It takes too long to clear all the windows, so you have to cut up just enough to see the road semi-adequately. It was fine. Everyone in Buffalo knows they're signed up for dangerous driving. I think a lot of us wouldn't mind dying in a brutal car accident. Nice and quick, unlike the slow torturous death of hypothermia.

Sheila started fine. She always did somehow. I hit the heat and sat there a moment, huffing hot smoky breath into my paralyzed fingers. I was going to my boy Frank's house. Frank and I were in business together. We sold weed.

I threw Sheila into reverse, and she crunched the snow beneath her and fell backward down the driveway quite lazily. Getting out was easier than getting in, usually. Momentum and shit.

By the time I was at the end of Pheasant Run, some of the ice on the windshield had melted. It was making the glass all translucent. You can't hit the wipers just yet. They'll certainly be frozen in place. You can still see on-coming traffic through a blurry windshield. It's like driving without your glasses—more challenging, but doable.

♦♦♦

I pulled up in front of Frank's house. It was well-kempt but plain. Plain as could be. I swore his parents both had a frontal lobotomy or some shit. I'd known Frank for, like, ten years, and

I'd probably had a full conversation with his folks, like, ten times total. I don't know. They were strange.

I texted him, *Here*.

He said, *Just come in*.

Nobody rang doorbells anymore.

I was finally warm, and now I had to step out into the cold and lose it all. Such was this life. I opened Sheila's door, which made a horrible cracking sound like it always did. The street was slush and salt. Black, nasty snow chunks along the side. Urban winters ain't no fuckin' wonderland.

Frank's little-ass schnauzers were hollerin' at me before I even opened the garage door. They were always hollerin' and yippin'. I like dogs, but not when they holler and yip. They were named Salt and Pepper—the schnauzers—and they calmed down once they sniffed my legs. I patted them on the head and whatnot.

When I opened the door to the house, the little bastards bolted between my legs and went inside. Frank's mom was standing there. I was all like, "Oh sorry. Is it okay if they come in?"

She stared at me, all plain-like, emotionless, for two seconds. It felt like ten. Then she said, "Oh yeah, that's fine."

It was little things like that with his parents. Moments of silence, like a dusty robot processing its response. I don't know. With a normal person, I would've asked how they were or something like that, but I didn't even bother.

Frank was upstairs in his room playing Xbox, the bowl of his bong still smoking. I sat down beside him. Gunshots were popping from the TV, and he was mumbling curses under his breath. Frank always liked the competition when it came to things not worth doing. At least that's how I saw it. He got angrier about badminton than he did about money. One of those. Racket thrower.

I took the bong and ripped a hefty one. Made me cough like a motherfucker. Still choking, I said, "Is this the shit?"

"Yeah," said Frank. He was hyper-focused on the TV.

"Where's the rest?"

"In the bag back there."

Beside his pile of clothes and an unhung poster of Sinatra's mugshot was a shitty old backpack. Inside was one pound of weed, sealed neatly in a Ziploc freezer bag. Some of the chunks were the size of baseballs. They rested atop the smaller nuggets, then the shake beneath that. Like a terrarium or some shit. I don't know.

Frank's player made an exhausted sigh, then died. Frank said, "Motherfucker. That's so fuckin' stupid. How could he even see me?"

I was in awe of this sack of marijuana. We'd never picked up a pound before. Business was doing well. So, I was all like, "How can you be upset in times like these?"

He said nothing. Everyone in my life seemed to be saying nothing. I was still happy though. I tossed the bag up into the air and caught it, all smiley, like it was a fuckin' baby.

"Where's the scale at?" I asked.

Frank was distracted. He was talking through the headset, saying, "They're up top! They're up top!" or some shit like that.

"Yo," I said.

"What?"

"Where's the scale at?"

"It's in the bag, too."

I took the crusty piece of equipment and the red Solo cup that lay with it. I fell back into the couch and ripped open that beautiful bag of herb. Earthy, skunky fragrance. Lovely. I hit the scale on, making it ignite blue. I placed the cup on it, then zeroed it out.

"You got another bag?" I asked.

"Uh," said Frank, focused on that fuckin' TV.

I was all like, "……"

"Uh, no," he said.

"Go get one, bitch."

"They're in the pantry. Just go get it."

"Bro, I'm not getting a baggie from your pantry."

"Dude, who cares. Just go."

"Your mom's down there."

"Dude, so. She doesn't care."

I was all like, "Oh my God." This was typical Frank. But he was right. Who cared?

They knew what we were up to—Frank's parents. They just didn't seem to have the courage to say anything. Or maybe they were cool with it. I don't know. They might've been former hippies. Maybe that was why their brains were fried—all those acid trips, staring into the sun and whatnot.

So, I was kind of stoned from that bong rip. I went down there, and his mom was in the kitchen, flipping through a magazine or some shit. I smiled all weird and was like, "Just getting something from the pantry."

She said nothing, just looked at me.

I went into their pantry, which was stacked with typical suburbanite shit: mayonnaise, baked beans, a choice of cereals, a grocery bag overflowing with other grocery bags. I couldn't tell if I was just high or if the Ziploc bags weren't in there. I was analyzing each shelf, and I couldn't find the fuckin' things. Maybe they were behind something. I started shifting stuff around, digging inward and whatnot.

I started getting hot.

I was just about to give up, then his mom was suddenly behind me and all like, "What are you looking for?"

I jumped.

She said nothing, waiting for my response.

I tripped over my words. Smiling. Blushing. You know. I was all like, "Uh. Uh. Uh. I'm looking for a Ziploc bag."

"Oh, they're in here," she said. She crouched down and pulled out this plastic box that held baggies and tin foil and parchment paper—shit like that. She handed me a little baggie.

I said, "Thank you," even though I knew it was way too small. Then I went back upstairs all stiff-like. My heart was pumping in my wrists.

Of course, Frank wanted to pay attention to me now. He was all like, "Not a bag like that, you dipshit."

"It's what your mom gave me."

"Bro, why didn't you ask for a bigger one?"

"I was nervous."

"Oh my God, Bobby. Hold on." He threw off the headset and went downstairs and got the right bag.

After he came back to his game, I slapped the fat wad of wrinkly twenties and fifties on the coffee table. It fit well among the dirty bong and the ash and all the other drug paraphernalia. Frank's eyes went back on the TV. Hundreds of dollars in cash lay before him, but his eyes were on the TV.

◆◆◆

I was out the door with my half-pound of weed in my jacket pocket.

This freak motherfucker named Walter was hitting up my

phone. Twitchy guy. He was in the grade below me and Frank. Once he got out of high school, he started smoking a lot of weed—probably to calm his nerves. He certainly needed it. Just being in that motherfucker's presence gave me anxiety. It was like it radiated off him. But money's money.

So, he was texting me. Asking me when I'd re-up.

I got back to him. Told him to meet me at my house.

He said, *Okay, be there soon.*

♦♦♦

Now, this motherfucker lived all the way out in the Heights, but somehow, he was standing at my doorstep before I even got back. Something big and circular was in his hand, and at first, I thought it was a fuckin' unicycle, but then I realized it was just a bike tire.

Why the fuck did he have a bike tire?

It had started snowing, and now the driveway was stacked. I gunned Sheila forward, then swung her sharply. I was hoping that if I hit the driveway with enough speed, she'd plow forward. Unfortunately, it didn't work out as such. The front tires bucked up like a fuckin' stallion when they hit the bank, then the car halted in the icy dent. I hit the gas, and the tires whined but stayed in place, tossing slush behind them. Half of Sheila was in the driveway. Half of Sheila was protruding into the fuckin' street. I ran the gas again, really gunned it this time.

Nothing.

I was stuck.

Walter's freak ass came up to my window. I tried to roll down the window, but that was stuck, too. The ice. I hated this life.

Humans weren't supposed to live here. It was unnatural.

I opened the door, saying, "Hey Walter."

Trembling, he said, "Hey."

"How'd you get here so quickly?" I asked.

"Oh. I was just in the neighborhood."

This freak knew no one in the neighborhood other than me, but whatever.

I said, "All right, let me get my car unstuck, then we can go inside."

"I'm actually in a hurry," he said.

I'd made drug deals in less secretive places. It actually looked less suspicious, if anything. Young punks coming in and out of your house all day says nothing other than drug dealer. But talking to some twitchy fuck while your car is trapped in snow, halfway in the street? That doesn't look suspicious—that just looks weird.

"All right, how much you want?" I asked.

"Well...." he said.

I said, "...."

"How much will you give me for this bike tire?" He presented the bike tire.

I didn't know how to respond. I just let my mouth hang open.

"It's from a BMX bike. Mongoose. It's a nice tire."

"Bro, what am I gonna do with a fuckin' bike tire?"

"I don't know. You could sell it. It's worth at least fifty bucks."

"Then why don't you sell it?"

This motherfucker started getting even more twitchy. He kept looking behind himself as if something was coming for him. He was all like, "I'm in such a hurry man."

"Bro, I am not accepting a fuckin' bike tire."

"Can you front me, then?"

Fronting people was tricky business. If you lent out weed, it was usually a pain in the ass getting the money back. But building a rep as a dealer willing to front brings you customers. Tricky business. I gave him a chance, eye-balled a dub, and wrapped it in a receipt lying on Sheila's floor.

He thanked me profusely, then disappeared into the snow-flurried sidewalk, bike tire at his side.

♦♦♦

With that freak gone, I was left alone with my stuck car. I hit the gas again as if it'd be any different this time. The tires spun and spun, but Sheila stayed put.

I threw her into reverse, gunned it, then threw her into drive, gunned it. Then again. And again. This is called the rocking method or something like that. It often works pretty well. I got Sheila maybe an inch or two forward after doing ten rotations of this. She sounded like her engine was gonna fuckin' blow if I pushed her any harder, though.

The wind was now hollerin' like gigantic ghosts. When I got out, it was biting at my ears. I peeked under Sheila, and her whole underbelly was lying atop a mound of ice and snow. That shit was thicker than I predicted, but I should've known. Those fuckin' plows. I mean, I'm thankful for them, I really am. But they pack the curbs so tightly it's like you're pulling into a wall of rock.

I took a shovel from the garage and tried to dig the tires free. All the while the snow was clumping everywhere. My face was wet and hurting. The shovel was hard plastic and could only do so much. It didn't have a sharp spade-like shape. Not right for this task. I tried to poke at the ice with its side, then yank loose the chopped snow. It sort of worked.

I got back in and rocked Sheila back and forth, back and forth, with no progress. This shit was a nightmare. The hogs certainly wouldn't be understanding of me leaving my car halfway in the street. It'd be a two-hundred-dollar fine, easily. I had to free Sheila.

♦♦♦

Ma was at the kitchen counter having a vodka and Tang. This was her go-to drink. She called it a White Trash Mimosa. And of course, she was smoking a Marb Light, too.

I was all snowy and flustered. I went to the lazy Susan with my sloshy boots still on.

Ma was all like, "Bobby, take your boots off. Shit."

I took the biggest pot from the lazy Susan. "I'm gonna be in and out," I said.

She exhaled smoke, whistled a little, ashed the cigarette in a coffee cup, then said, "What's going on?"

"My car's stuck."

She took her White Trash Mimosa to the window and peered. "Shit, Bobby, you're halfway in the street."

"I know," I said, all annoyed-like.

I put the pot under the sink and hit the faucet to the hot side.

Ma was all like, "What the hell are you doing?"

"I'm gonna try and melt the tires free."

"Bobby, that's not gonna work."

"Why not?"

"It's too cold."

"It's worth a shot. Nothing else is working."

I felt the water, and it wasn't even lukewarm. Of course. I dumped it into the sink, then placed it under there again.

"Did you hear what I said earlier about the bathtub?" I asked.

"I saw," she said.

"It looks like it's about to fall through the floor."

"Well," she said, passively, hoping the problem would just float away.

In a past life, my mom was a nurse. Now she was a drinker. Most of her drinking money came from her boyfriends. My dad paid off the mortgage long ago with cash acquired through illegal means. I paid the utilities. It was a hard life, but she couldn't give me any shit about dealing because it was the only thing keeping the heat on. And in Buffalo, you die if the heat isn't on.

So, the pot was full and steaming. I shut off the sink and picked it up by its handles. Fucker was heavy. Hard to keep level, but I was determined. A lot was at stake. If I spilled this, I might scald myself for life.

I was all like, "Ma, get the door."

She huffed but complied.

The hot water was splashing in the pot as I stepped outside. The snow smacking my face was sharp and determined, and it discombobulated my flustered ass. Just one fuckin' foot down the steps was all it took. My leg flew in front of me, and I slipped backward. I smacked my head, and suddenly the world above me looked like puddles. I came to after a second. Three giant icicles were wobbling above me. They dinged like a windchime of death. The boiling water spilled all over my jacket, soaked through the zipper, and finally penetrated my skin. It wasn't that bad. The jacket took most of it, but I still cursed and pulled the soaking fabric from my body.

I sat upright, in defeat. Ma was behind me asking if I was all right.

I said nothing.

♦♦♦

Ma's boyfriend had a truck, and he pulled Sheila free an hour later. Gerald was the dude's name. Black guy. After my dad went to the pokey, my mom seemed to only have a thing for darker-skinned men.

Maybe this is a good point to bring this up: it wasn't normal to have a dad in prison for murder in my neighborhood. I grew up in Buffalo, but not in the boondocks or anything. I lived in a white trash neighborhood, but it was still the suburbs, nonetheless. Most of my friends' parents were mechanics or servers or some shit like that. Welfare for some, too. But none were a motorcycle outlaw. My dad was the outlier, and it haunted me most of my life. I knew kids' parents told them about my dad. Word got around. I hated it when I was younger.

But now, being in the drug trade myself, my father's crimes did nothing but aid me. I was of pristine pedigree, and as in all disciplines, which meant something. No one ever directly said it, but I knew they talked about these things when I wasn't there: *Yeah, you know that Bobby Washburn kid? Yeah, his dad killed someone. He was in a motorcycle gang or some shit. Yeah, don't mess with that Bobby kid. He's got killer in his blood.*

That's what they said. I was sure of it.

♦♦♦

Afterward, Gerald cooked me and Ma dinner. She was all fucked up. She said, "Bobby, I love you, yous know that, right?"

"Yes, Ma. Love you, too."

"All right. I was juss making sure."

Now she was drinking box wine. White Trash Mimosas by day, box wine by night. Frankly, I don't know what Gerald saw in her. The dude kind of had his shit together. Kind of. He was, like, fifty years old and working at Bob Evans. A manager, though.

He laid the plate of macaroni and vodka sauce before Ma.

She said, "Thank you, baby," all drunk-like. She made some incoherent joke about the vodka sauce getting her drunk and laughed to herself, slapped her knee, and shit. It was hard to watch. I didn't have the energy to smile anymore. Ma could actually be pretty funny when she was sober, but she was pretty much never sober.

Gerald put a plate before me. "Thanks, man," I said.

"You're welcome," he said.

It wasn't, like, homemade vodka sauce or anything, I should add. It came out of a jar, but it was still pretty good. While I ate, I could hear Ma struggling. She could be like a fuckin' toddler when she was drunk. I didn't grant her the attention.

Gerald sat down, too. He was gonna grant her the attention. He always did. Idiot.

She was eating all sloppy-like, and Gerald said, "Carol."

Then she said, "What? What?"

"Stop," he said.

"Stop what? Stop what? The macaroni is too soft. Why did you make it soft if you knew I'd struggle with it? Why?"

I laughed at that.

Gerald was like, "What does that even mean?"

She swooped her head swift and low and bit the macaroni from Gerald's fork, like some sort of predatory bird on a field mouse.

"Oh my God," he said.

She started laughing, then was all like, "What? What? You're so grouchy. You made the good kind for yourself, so I took it."

He started ignoring her. Then she put her hand on his shoulder, all serious-like, saying, "Are you mad at me? Baby, are you mad at me?"

Gerald stared straight ahead, not looking left or right.

Ma said, "Whatever," then took four audible glugs of wine, her throat moving up and down.

Something was wrong thereafter. She brought the cup down slowly. I could see the concern in her eyes. She tried to act normal, but clearly couldn't. Her throat throbbed a bit, and her lips pursed. She brought her hand to her mouth, then said, "Buuuuuuuuuuh," and vomited a quart of chunky wine through her fingers and onto her plate.

Gerald stood up, freaking out, going, "Jesus Christ! Oh my God, Carol! Jesus!"

He put his hand to his mouth, too. Gagged a bit. He was one of those wimps who vomited when he saw other people vomit. He booked it out of the room, all goofy-like. Guy wasn't particularly athletic. I could hear him hollerin' into the toilet bowl, muttering angry testaments in between each fit.

Ma had wine dripping down her mouth and forearm. It looked like blood. She closed her eyes and laid her head beside the plate. Time for sleep, I guess. The puddle of puke slightly rippled as she breathed.

I finished eating in silence. The smell was horrible.

◆◆◆

That night, I stored my weed in my lock box. In there, is my collection of all things sinful. The remnants of medicine cabinet thefts: Adderalls, Vyvanses, Ambiens, Percocets, Tramadols, some other generic brand tablets I'd long forgotten the desired effect of. A little vial of hash. Two scales caked in residue. Some shitty cocaine. Long expired condoms. Knives. Three tabs of some research chemical advertised as LSD at a Kid Cudi concert. A little sack of synthetic pot called Mr. Happy. Brass knuckles. A throwing-star I found at the flea market. But no gun. Getting approved for a pistol permit in New York was like getting accepted into Cornell.

◆◆◆

I slept till the next afternoon. My bedsheets were ripe. My room was messy. I lay in the filth and trinkets like some lonely hermit. I fiddled through my phone until I felt active enough to rise. The second the blankets were off me, I was cold. The windows in my room were aged. There were still fuckin' wolves in New York when this house was built, damn near.

I walked to the sunken shower and turned it on. It was nerve-wracking standing in that death trap, but I was getting used to it. I bathed, then shaved in the steamy mirror. My steamy phone had some texts. Clients. Folks needed their weed. Usually, I'd make the effort to go to them, but on that day, I just wasn't feeling it. I said, *Come through.*

I put my pajamas back on, fired up the scale, weighed out the dime bags and eighths, and waited for them to come through.

I complained a lot, certainly, but this was a good life.

♦♦♦

Come night, Frank was picking me up to head to the bar. Slick Willy's. It was where everyone went.

The place was crowded with the basic-ass patrons I'd come to expect. Comb-over and tattooed boys in untucked button-downs. Girls in shiny little dresses even though it was like ten fucking degrees out. Either Taylor Swift, trap music, or "Don't Stop Believing" was blaring from the speakers. White people shit. There was a hint of diversity, though. The University of Buffalo had a lot of Asians. The Asians were on the rise in Buffalo's underworld. They loved money and drugs just as any other race did.

Frank and I went to the bar. As soon as the bartender saw us, he came over. We knew the guy. Elephantine motherfucker named Thanassis. Family name. Greek, I think.

"What's up," he said, placing his big-ass hands on the bar.

"Sup, Thanassis," I said.

"What'll it be?"

Frank and I both ordered a shot of well whiskey and a Heineken. I tipped the man well. We both did. With cash came charity. Don't get it twisted though: my money was largely a facade. I mean, I did okay, but weed dealing only gave off the illusion that I was loaded. I always had a lot of cash, and everyone around me always seemed to be giving me more cash. I probably made, like, thirty a year, though. Maybe less. I don't know. A huge chunk of the money was just breaking even. The public didn't need to know that, though. As far as they were concerned, I was the richest motherfucker in the neighborhood.

Frank and I took our shots, then hit our Heineken. We put our backs to the bar and watched the grimy circus before us. Cliques of bros and chicks hollered with the song. There were plenty of people I recognized from high school. I'd probably talk to a few of them once I was more liquored up.

In the back, there were rows of pool tables that were often neglected on nights when there were girls about. Frank and I went back there and slapped hands with some punks from the neighborhood. Decent enough dudes. We talked about nothing worth mentioning, then played a round of pool.

I was never good at pool. I always preferred darts, but it was hard to play darts in a crowded bar. Some drunk motherfuckers might casually pass by just as you let go and get his eye harpooned.

♦♦♦

We grew significantly drunker. Certainly. We drank well.

Frank's grouchy-ass was maddoggin' all night.

I was all like, "What?"

He kept that serious stare.

"What?" I asked.

"It's that Asian motherfucker again," he said.

I looked across the bar and caught a glimpse of the guy we had beef with. He tried giving us trouble for selling weed at a party about a week ago. It was just typical, drunk-man ego shit. I was over it, but Frank wasn't. He didn't like to be disrespected. I guess I didn't mind it.

So, this kid was dressed in expensive jeans and an Adidas sweater. Diamond earrings. Gold bracelet. They called this motherfucker A-Rod, which was pathetic. As if he was murdering people—big hitter. Get it?

Regardless of his phony-ass shit, the dude had a pretty big network up at the University of Buffalo. But he was actually just the underboss. The Asian kingpin was actually a queenpin, named Leslie. She was rarely seen and apparently packed lips. Bizarre, I know. An Asian girl named Leslie is a drug lord and chews tobacco. There are a lot of bizarre legends in the drug underworld, just nobody writes books about them. That's why God put me here, I suppose.

A-Rod was in a circle of folks that didn't appear to be his posse. Posses give off a certain stance. These chicks and bros weren't giving it off. Frank kept glaring at this motherfucker like a pit bull on a squirrel. The alcohol was only aiding his fury.

At some point, we were out in the snow smoking a cigarette with this girl named Nora. Frank was flirting with her, and she was giving it right back. All smiley-like, the both of them. I just stood there drunk and smoked my boge, shaking. They say alcohol keeps you warm. Not in Buffalo. I was still cold. I was trying to hide my trembling, but I couldn't.

Frank was maddoggin' again.

From the pizza place beside Slick's came A-Rod. He was biting into steaming hot slices from a paper plate. He came up to us, met eyes with Frank, smiled, then said, "What's good?" all friendly-like. A genuine friendly. Not a testing friendly.

Frank then smiled, too. They slapped hands as if suddenly all the hard feelings vanished just by coming into contact with each other. They apologized and talked for some time. A-Rod's mouth was greasy and sloppy with pizza. Frank's grin was seemingly sincere.

I was suspicious, and it all came clear when Frank said, "Yo, can we get some bud off you? We actually just went dry." This would imply fealty. The man you get the weed from is above you.

A-Rod was all like, "No doubt, my man. Here, take my number."

They made the exchange on their phones, then slapped each other's hands once again. Then A-Rod returned to the bar.

Frank's face became evil. "I'm gonna rob that motherfucker," he said, and he made sure Nora heard it.

♦♦♦

At home, all the inside lights were on. I found Ma on the couch, snoring, lit cigarette between her fingers, the ash long and bent and shriveled like a dead man's finger. I took it, and the ash fell. I cleaned up a bit. Turned off the lights. Guzzled water before I went to bed.

I had stopped putting a blanket over her a while ago.

♦♦♦

I was only a little hungover the next morning. I was still young enough where it could work that way. Sundays were good for business because a lot of folks needed their weed to kill the hangover. I already had a few texts.

I was in Sheila, smoking a joint. This punk named Geoff was the last of those few texts I had. He needed an eighth, and of course, I complied. We pronounced it Gee-off, I should add, which was quite rude, but we did things that were quite rude all the time.

The Bills were playing one of their final games of the season. They weren't going to the playoffs, of course. Down these snowy suburban streets were the homes of working-class folks with Irish or Italian or Polish blood. This was the day of the week for family and God and remote controls flying through TVs and Labatt Blues. Many.

Gee-off lived in these apartments down in the Willow Ridge area. There were drunk college students in Zubaz and red wigs and bison horn helmets, drinking beers and smoking cigarettes beside a fire pit. Barbarous, us Buffalonians. I pulled up to them. I said, "You guys need some weed?"

They did. So, I sold them some weed. Gave them my number.

I had to drive back and forth through the whole fuckin' parking lot before I found Gee-off's. I hated apartment complexes for that reason. I'm sure pizza delivery boys had to deal with the same shit. We had a similar occupation.

The sun was blaring from above, so it wasn't too bad out. The floor of the parking lot was filthy water. The high piles of snow reflected the sunlight like white mirrors.

The apartment's lobby had that smell of antique mildew as they always do. Before I reached 5A, I could hear them hollerin'. I knocked with a melody. That's a courtesy of the underworld. The hogs never knock with a melody. They pound.

Some kid I didn't recognize opened the door. He was all smiley-like, beer on his breath, and said, "Sup, man!"

He let me in.

The Bills game was radiating from the TV. The room was filled with guys who were nobodies in high school, but then went to college and had their first beer and built a new layer of confidence. Look at how petty I sound. I dropped out of college.

Gee-off stood and was like, "Yo, what's up, Bobby," as if we were old friends. He slapped me up. I smiled all polite-like. I was pretty judgmental on the inside, but not on the surface. Bad for business.

I gave him the eighth, and he gave me two twenties. I returned a five. Thirty-five for an eighth was a good price. We could do things like that now that we were picking up by the pound. I was still profiting quite well, too.

This annoying-ass motherfucker was all like, "What's its name?" when he examined the bag.

I was like, "Huh?" all-smiley on the surface.

He said, "I just had some lemon kush the other day and that shit was mad strong, yo."

These fuckin' fairies. Ever since that movie *Pineapple Express* came out, every idiot thought weed had different names. I mean, I'm sure it did, but it was just made up by some dealers like me. The only difference was those dealers had time on their hands to come up with stupid shit like that.

"It's called weed," I said.

He was all like, "Oh, ha-ha, yeah, word."

Freak. I was trying to get out of this sausage fest but Gee-off's bitch-ass kept going, like, "Come on, Bobby, have a beer. Have a beer."

I agreed but immediately regretted it. A drug dealer should be good at saying no to people. I was not.

Gee-off gave me a chilled bottle of Labatt and I twisted the cap free. Drank. We sat around on couches and wooden chairs and watched the Bills trail at halftime. These fuckers were mad obnoxious and cringy. I glugged that beer down and built some liquid courage and said my goodbyes. That's what I liked about alcohol—it made me much more willing to do shit I wanted to do.

♦♦♦

So, once I had one beer, I couldn't just stop there. I never understood people who did that. Let's not get this twisted—alcohol is a drug, and I used it as such. You wouldn't just take a puff of weed and call it a night. I found it stranger to have just one glass of wine with dinner instead of the whole bottle.

Back home, Ma and Gerald were watching the Bills continue to lose. They were both drinking Mike's Hard Lemonade. Gerald brought it. He only drank girly shit like that.

They were sitting awkwardly on the couch. They were close but not touching. Maybe, like, three inches apart, as if they were teenagers on their first movie date—clearly into each other, but too nervous to touch. Bear in mind these two adults had been dating for, like, a year.

"Can I have one of those?" I said, pointing to the Mike's.

"Sure. They're in the fridge," said Gerald.

Ma was just slouching, sunglasses on.

I took one of the yellow and black cans from the fridge. They were actually Mike's Harders which were, like, 8% alcohol or something like that. Basically wine. I cracked it and took multiple long hits. Half burped. You know, like those really airy burps, but not a full one. I made fun of Mike's, but it was honestly pretty good.

I sat down on the couch with them. A tight squeeze now. All my life the Bills were losing. We didn't speak, the three of us. We just watched the fuzzy television, sipped our drinks until we were drunk. The time ticked to the two-minute warning, then soon to 0:00. It was a numb drunk. To ease.

◆◆◆

Some days later, I was back at Frank's, and he was all like, "So you ready?"

"Ready for what?" I asked.

"To rob that Asian motherfucker."

I thought that was just drunken boasting, but now, even in a sober state days later, Frank had vengeance in his fists. He was always like that. Every score had to be settled with him, even when we were children. When he was wronged in any way, his anger would never dissipate, but instead, quietly grow until he was violent.

Anyway, this put me in a spot, you know? It felt like it was primarily Frank's quarrel, and he was just dragging me into it, but if I were to say no, I'd be a bitch. If you're a drug dealer, you don't want to be a punk-ass bitch. Suburbs or the trap, you don't want that.

So, I tried talking him out of it with slippery shit, saying it was bad for business and things of that nature. But Frank wasn't having it. No sir. He said, "I'm robbing this motherfucker with or without you."

His confidence actually comforted me. I'd been in some street fights, but it wasn't like I was some hardened warrior. That shit was still scary. A-Rod wasn't intimidating physically, but who knew, maybe that nickname wasn't bullshit after all. Maybe we would get our taints handed to us.

"How do you wanna do it?" I asked.

So, this motherfucker reaches his hand under his bed. His smile was that of a ten-year-old showing me some shit he's not supposed to have, like matches or dirty magazines. But we were twenty-two now, and Frank, to my surprise, pulled out a fuckin' pistol.

"Jesus Christ," I said.

He put it to his head and pulled the trigger. It made a plastic snap, then he smiled. "It's fake," he said.

It was one of those high-end airsoft guns, but with the orange tip ripped off. It looked real. I held it. It felt real.

"Damn," I said.

"So, you ready?"

◆◆◆

We waited for A-Rod in some apartment complex parking lot. Above us, construction workers were installing a window. Frank had the heat blowing and Christmas music playing from the radio. We both liked Christmas music. The more traditional stuff, you know? Not that "Dominic the Christmas Donkey" bullshit. We never discussed our mutual enjoyment of "Deck the Halls." But neither of us protested when things of the like were on the radio. Silent agreement.

We tracked A-Rod from afar until he reached the car. Frank turned off the radio, and we watched this ill-fated man grab the handle. There was haste in his step. He was hurrying to escape the cold.

He opened the back door and got in, bringing a huff of freezing air with him. He had a little drawstring bag in his hands. "Yo," he said, sort of out of breath.

"Sup," we said in unison.

A-Rod's smile fell. Just like that, he recognized that something wasn't right here. It was in the air. That aura of danger.

But before he could react, Frank pulled the fake gat from his coat and pointed it at A-Rod. There was a moment of silence thereafter. A-Rod stared down the barrel—not in disbelief, but some unusual acceptance, like it had happened before, like he was accustomed to it.

He said, "Shoot me."

Now the aura of danger was shared by all of us. Okay, maybe we misjudged this A-Rod guy. Yes. We certainly did.

Frank pulled the gun away and got out of the car. He closed the door behind him, leaving me and A-Rod to an awkward moment of eye contact.

He looked at me confused.

I said, "Uh."

Then he tried to run.

Frank was at the door faster. He was damn near foaming at the mouth. He whipped the gun at A-Rod, and it clunked his noggin with a horrible crack. Then Frank started punching him. A-Rod held up his hands to block the blows, and he scooched over to escape out the other side.

That's when I got out and caught him. I took hold of his collar, but he spun around and molliwopped the side of my head, making my brain ring. I threw some poor jabs, catching him on the shoulders or missing altogether. Frank turned into a linebacker and tackled A-Rod's ass into the snow. The two of them were grunting and rolling around like fighting dogs. A-Rod had the drawstring gripped tightly against his chest, leaving his face exposed to Frank's horrible elbows. The crack at my head had me dizzy, so I started kicking his ankles. I don't know. I guess I was trying to disable his legs so he couldn't run away. I felt his femur vibrate every time I landed a good one.

The beaten man started gurgling promises through his bloody mouth. He said he was going to kill us. He said it again. Cursing us. So, Frank jawed him real good and started tugging at the drawstring bag. A-Rod wasn't letting go. The two of them had this tug-a-war while I rocked his legs until they were raw. Frank dropped another elbow, and A-Rod finally released his grip to try and block the blow. Frank tossed the bag back to me, and I didn't catch it. It would've looked cooler if I caught it, but I didn't. I picked it up and put it in the car.

A-Rod looked borderline unconscious. Frank stood, sucking in huge breaths. He was soaked in dirty slush, accented by blood. He grabbed A-Rod by the hair, making the poor guy squeal, then mugged him for any cash. He threw the empty wallet into the snow. Suddenly, the side of my head hurt like a motherfucker.

The construction workers were hanging there, watching us. Frank, who was still panting, looked at the guys, smiled, and waved with his blood-soaked hand. They waved back all timid-like.

A-Rod lay there in the fetal position. He was breathing weirdly. Moaning weirdly. Almost whispering.

Frank and I got back in the car. He turned the Christmas music back on, and we got the fuck out of there.

♦♦♦

I could feel my heartbeat in the side of my head come morning. It felt like there was a massive lump there, but there wasn't. I stared at myself in the freezing morning mirror. There was just a slight scrape, like a brush-burn. The phantom lump still pulsed though.

It was an ounce we stole from A-Rod. Frank and I split it halfway. Now a free half-ounce of weed was pretty nice. On top of my half-pound, that was like extra two-hundred bucks. When selling weed, a huge chunk of your cash was just the money you earned back to break even. But if you robbed a motherfucker, there was no breaking even. It was all profit.

Ma was knocking shit over downstairs. Soon she was all like, "BOBBY! BOBBY!" as if she was getting murdered.

I ran down there, ready to crack fuckin' skulls, going, "What! What! What!"

She was just casually sitting at the kitchen table, all languid-like. She said, "We're going to Bob Evans. Get ready."

"Jesus, Ma."

"What?"

"I thought you were dying or something."

"Oh," she said, sipping her White Trash Mimosa. "Sorry, hun."

"Why are we going to Bob Evans?" I asked. I wasn't really protesting. There was just such certainty in her tone, it was perplexing.

"Because," she said. "Gerald gave me this free breakfast certificate."

"Oh. Can he do that?"

She was suddenly offended. "Of course, he can, Bobby. He loves me. Did you not know that?"

♦♦♦

She had her White Trash Mimosa in the car with her. The tumbler was filled to the fuckin' brim, and it kept spilling at every bump, and she'd go, "Whoops!"

"Ma, stop spilling it."

"Well, quit driving like a maniac."

I was driving like the next man, but it wasn't worth fighting over.

"Now my hand's all sticky," she said. "Thanks, Bobby."

"Oh my God," I said quietly. That's all there was to do—ask the mighty one for some divine fuckin' intervention.

I pulled Sheila into the Bob Evans' parking lot which was black and salty and speckled with the vehicles of the elderly: Buicks, Lincolns. I shut Sheila off, and Ma was examining my cupholders which were full of loose shit. "Where can I put this?" she asked.

"I don't know, Ma," I said, all annoyed-like.

"Wow, Bobby," she said. She threw some of the garbage into the back seat and set the sticky glass down. I was too tired to protest. Now my whole head hurt.

Ma wrapped her arm around mine as we walked in. The two of us: mother and son—one drunk, the other wounded from a drug robbery—on their way to free pancakes. That was the greatest display of white trash I think one could see. Picturesque, really.

The interior of Bob Evans looked like an IHOP that was in a basement. Dark and shadowy. That smell of nursing home and butter. The air was hot and motionless. I saw Gerald's dorky ass standing right there at the counter, addressing his employees or some shit. He noticed us and gave a head nod. Ma blew him a kiss, and it was discomforting for everyone, including the host. She just quickly brought us to a booth and handed us the menus.

I was in the mood for pancakes, but I didn't really like getting pancakes because I could just make them at home. It wasn't like Bob Evan's recipe tasted any better than Aunt Jemima's. I preferred to get something I would never take the time to make at home, like hash browns and sausage and whatnot. You feel me?

Our waiter was this preppy motherfucker named Tanner or some shit. He asked us what he could get us started with to drink, all smiley-like. He had a combover.

"I'll have coffee please," I said.

He was all like, "Great, great," then scribbled into his stupid little notebook.

"I'll have a Manhattan, please," said Ma.

Thankfully, Tanner thought she was joking. He smiled and said, "Part of Bob Evans' ethos is an alcohol-free environment."

Ma got all snake-like at that. "Are you serious?" she asked.

"Yes, ma'am."

"Coffee's fine," she said. "Please."

"Great, great," he said. "Two coffees. All right. I'll go get those. Let me know if you have any questions with the menu." He was smiling.

Ma and I said "Thank you" at the same time.

I lifted my menu and browsed. It was laminated and painted in dazzling photographs of scrambled eggs and French toast and fresh fruit and the like. I heard Ma rustling with something, and I tried to ignore it until I couldn't ignore it anymore. I peered over the laminated pancake stack that protruded from the menu to see Ma struggling to unscrew a flask.

"Always have a backup, Bobby," Ma said.

I rolled my eyes. I think the family of four parallel to us all did the same. Church-looking motherfuckers.

"God, you have to be fuckin' Hercules to get these things open," she mumbled.

"Ma," I said.

"What?"

"Could you at least be a little discreet?"

"Maybe if it weren't so fuckin' hard to get open."

She continued her stuck twist on the cap, her face all red and squinted.

I tried to ignore her, but once again I could only withstand it for so long.

"Oh my God, Ma. Give it to me."

She passed me the pink, beaded flask underneath the table. I took hold of the thing and tried to rip it open. She was right. It was fuckin' hard to get open.

"Did you super glue this?" I asked.

"I don't think so."

It was kind of hard to get a nice grip on the thing while holding it under the table. My arms were shoved against the edge. I handed it back to Ma and said, "You'll just have to wait till we get home."

"Come on, Bobby," she said. "Be a man."

"The thing's fuckin' tight," I said. "Here, give it back to me."

"No, no, just forget it."

"Give it to me."

Gerald approached us boss-man-like. Before he could even speak, Ma flashed the flask upright and said, "Here, Gerald, show Bobby how a man opens a flask."

He snatched it from her and hid it in his pocket. He looked around to see who noticed. All the old people nearby were looking. Old people love to talk shit, so they keep their eyes peeled for stuff like this. Gerald smiled at them all painful-like.

He snapped back to Ma. "Jesus Christ, Carol, you can't have that in here."

"Why not? It's a free fuckin' country."

"Alcohol is against Bob Evans' ethos," he said.

Ma was all like, "So you're the one who coined that? I thought Talon over there was just a freak."

I laughed at that one.

"Carol," he said. "Please, not here."

"What Gerald? Am I embarrassing you?"

"Yes, you are. This is my job, Carol."

"Oh, I'm embarrassing you, am I? Well, sorry I'm so embarrassing Mr. Manager of Bob Evans. Sorry, I'm just such a bother to you and all your fine employees named after chicken feet."

Gerald sighed. I felt bad for the guy, but I was enjoying this show. His eyes were closed in frustration, and he said, "Are you two ready to order?"

Ma opened a menu. "Oh God, I haven't even looked yet," she said. "Bobby, you go first."

Gerald looked at me. I was all like, "Uh. I'll just have the tall stack."

Ma lowered her menu. "No, Bobby, don't get pancakes. I can just make you pancakes at home. Get something we don't get at home."

She was right, but for some reason, I fought her on it. I was all like, "I want pancakes."

Gerald was all like, "Let the boy have pancakes if he wants pancakes."

"Fine, fine," said Ma under her breath. "Just a waste is all."

She ordered a number three or some shit. Would likely eat none of it. Gerald just wrote it down in his head and went to leave for the kitchen.

Ma was like, "Gerald."

And he was like, "What?"

She presented her hand. "The flask," she said.

♦♦♦

The weather was horrible for days. The sky was disgraced with such residual storm clouds, it was as if it was always dusk. The wooden fingers of trees mauled the roof and windows, desperately, like they were begging to get in, like they were begging for this small taste of warmth. When the wind came, it sounded like it came from a world different from this one. Primeval, perhaps. Stuck in some unremembered cavern until now.

I sat in my room all day and smoked weed and jerked off.

♦♦♦

The blizzard hardly let up. The snow piled over the windows, and just like that, we were buried in our own house. I dipped into my collection of drugs. Vyvanse, 80 mg. It made me yearn to play some video games I hadn't played in years. They weren't even fun. I was just so incredibly fixated. I did this for hours, then started to feel the comedown. The comedown always makes it not worth it. I would just forget that. Amphetamines do two things: they make you really want to do something, and they make whatever it is that you're doing really interesting. Now, see, the former lasts quite a while, but the latter doesn't. You reach this state where you're so fuckin' hyperactive, but absolutely nothing in the world seems appealing. That's what we call the comedown. The only solution is to counter it with a downer of some sort.

I went downstairs. Ma was slumped on the couch, a stalactite of drool hanging from her lips. I said, "Ma," semi-softly.

And she responded with something incoherent with her eyes still closed. The drool splatted into the rug and was gone. She returned to her drunken sleep with a snort.

I figured I'd give one of her White Trash Mimosas a try. I took a spoonful of Tang and a spoonful of sugar and placed it in a coffee mug. I think Tang was the reason I always pronounced orangutan orangutang. The commercials always had one of those potbellied monkeys drinking the stuff.

Ma drank Barton's Vodka, which was one step up from Nikolai. I poured two fingers and swirled it all together. I took a hit, and it wasn't that bad. It was closer to a screwdriver than a mimosa, really, but mimosa sounded classier. I sipped at it and leaned against the counter. A ripple of depression went from my heart to my wrists. Typical comedown shit. I drank faster. On second thought, the White Trash Mimosa wasn't that great. It kind of tasted like vomit.

A pack of Pall Malls sat on the counter, too. Must've been Gerald's. Ma sure as hell didn't smoke Pall Malls. I pulled one free from the wrinkly packet and lit it with the stove. The drags of nicotine woke me up a bit, but only a bit. I'd have to reach a hefty level of inebriated to counter the bane of amphetamine comedown.

I kept on.

I hit the radio, and Sinatra was singing, "Have yourself a merry little Christmas." There was one Mike's Harder left over in the fridge, and I took that and drank it instead. It was better than the White Trash Mimosa. I poured a shot of straight Barton's and chased it with the lemonade. It was horrible, but at least short-lived.

After a few more, my belly started to feel snuggly. A huff of wind blew away the pile of snow blocking the window, and suddenly I could see the angelic snowfall on the cushiony world. I sat at the kitchen table with my drink, a fresh smoke, the music crackling, and watched.

♦♦♦

I woke to bangin'. I lifted my head from the kitchen table, the yellow light blaring over me. I'd fallen asleep on the side of my head that took the mollywop, and now it was seething in hurt.

The banging again. Someone was banging at the door.

I got up all dizzy-like. Ma woke, too, and she said, "Who the fuck's at the door in the middle of a blizzard?"

I unlatched the frozen lock from its place and ripped open the heavy door, the arctic breeze immediately pushing inward. There stood the back of a man. He turned around. It was the freak Walter.

This time he stood without his bike tire, only his huge coat and tuk and scarf and snow pants that puffed outward in great insulation.

"Hey, Bobby," he said behind his scarf.

I sighed. "What are you doing here?"

"I was wondering if I could get some weed off you?"

"Jesus Christ."

Ma was hollering, "Bobby, who is it?"

I said to Walter, "Dude, you came all the way over here in the storm?"

Remember, this motherfucker lived in a different neighborhood. The freezing air was getting to me already.

He said, "I couldn't wait any longer."

"Why didn't you text me?" I asked.

"I lost your number."

Ma asked again, "Bobby, who is it?"

"Jesus Christ, Ma. Just a friend."

I looked back at Walter. He was standing there all pathetic, trembling like a lost puppy. How could I possibly turn him away?

So, I was like, "All right, get on in here."

"Thanks, Bobby," he said.

Of course, once again, this motherfucker came to me without any money. He was going on and on about how he was getting paid in the morning and that he'd get the dough to me right at the ass crack of dawn. I'd heard that before, too many times. Seriously. That exact promise. Nearly every pothead wanting me to front them was apparently getting paid in the morning. But not once— truly not a single time—had I heard from them the following morning. I always had to hound them. Maybe Walter would be the one exception, but I doubted it. Then again, he did walk to my house in a fuckin' blizzard.

I tried to not let these things get to me. Life is too short to lose sleep over freaks like Walter. Too short to fume over thirty-five dollars. You can write that on my tombstone.

So, me and this dude sat in my room and ripped the bowl free of charge. We watched the Sabres game. The Sabres were looking decent that year. Better than the Bills, but that wasn't saying much. Even when this motherfucker was stoned, he was still so skittish. Every slapshot made him jump in his seat. It made me jump, too. I peed a little in my boxers.

I was feeling bold, so I said, "Walter if you don't mind me asking, what's wrong with you?"

"What do you mean?"

"You got anxiety or something?"

"Yeah," he said, all somber-like.

"Does the weed help?"

"Not really. It makes it worse sometimes."

"Why do you smoke it then?"

"I don't know. Feeling different is better than feeling how I normally do. Even if it's scary. If that makes any sense."

"I think it does," I said. "I think I know what you mean."

◆◆◆

I don't know if I believe in coincidences. A lot of the time, they felt like fate. The next day, I made a run to a regular named Debra. She was the manager at a local Tim Horton's. Middle-aged women, short hair, big thighs, smoked a lot of weed.

When I entered, she saw me and smiled. She was making a peppermint macchiato or some shit like that and hollered, "Give me one second, Bobby," across the café.

"All right," I said. I stood there with my hands in my jacket pockets, watching the miserable heads in front of me wait for their caffeine. Then I looked to my left and almost shit.

A-Rod.

He was sitting at a table, watching me. His face was all geared up and marred. Crusted cuts now dried black covered his forehead and lips. His eye was black. It was hardly open, but with the one healthy eye, he stared at me. He stared, and he didn't blink. I blinked.

I looked back to Debra, and she was still busy. I contemplated leaving. My survival instinct told me to flee, but my street instinct told me to stand firm.

I forced myself to maddog him back. I hadn't even noticed that he was with someone else until now. Asian girl with a fat lip. But this lip wasn't fat from bludgeoning—it was fat with a wad of dip. It was Leslie. The queenpin. The legends were true.

A-Rod said something like, "That's him."

She smiled slowly, exposing that soggy, black chunk of chew. She raised a finger gun, closed one eye, banged the hammer twice, at me.

"All right, Bobby," Debra hollered.

I walked past the line and went behind the counter and into the office like I always did. I was shaking.

Debra started chatting me up. "Bobby these customers are gonna make me lose my mind. Some lady flipped out on me today over eleven cents, and I couldn't handle it. I was about to explode. Meanwhile, we were wrapped in drive-thru and…"

"You got a back door?" I asked.

"What?"

I plopped the bag of weed on her lap. "Do you have a back door?"

"Yeah, through the bakery, why?"

I left.

"Wait, I didn't pay you," she said.

"Next time," I said, and was gone.

◆◆◆

When I came home, Ma was dressed nice. She had her signature thick red lipstick on. She would make a pact to get sober, and her first step was always to clean herself up nicely. It usually lasted twenty-four hours.

I stepped inside, huge coat and backpack on. Ma crushed her cigarette in the ashtray, the sparks dancing around her long, painted fingernails.

"Hi," I said.

"Hi," she said.

I slipped my Tims off and began to head upstairs.

Ma stopped me, saying, "Bobby, I've been thinking."

I was all like, "...."

"I think before Christmas, you should go see your father. I don't think he really gets any visitors anymore."

I hadn't seen the guy once in my adult life. We just stopped going. I don't know. We apparently used to go more when I was a kid, but I could hardly remember. I remembered the security guards and how they seemed so angry. I asked Ma if the security guard was my dad's friend. That made them laugh, but it was an uncomfortable laugh. Certainly uncomfortable. I don't know why I remember that, and only that, but I do.

I said, "All right. That's fine."

She nodded.

I went to leave again, and she said, "Bobby."

"What?"

"I love you."

"Love you, too."

♦♦♦

They had him out in Attica. That's a little town southeast of Buffalo, not known for much except its maximum-security prison. When I typed it into the GPS, I was expecting it to say three hours or something. I thought it was way out there in the middle of New York, out by the Finger Lakes, and what have you. It was actually more like forty-five minutes. All my life I hadn't known he was so close.

I probably should've checked Sheila's oil before a drive like this, but I didn't. The tire pressure light was on, so I probably should've looked into that, too, but I didn't. It was too cold. Always too cold. I'd do it in the summer. Yes, in the summer.

The highways out to the east of New York turn to long country roads. The landscape there is of planes of snow with the dead stalks of yesterspring's harvest protruding out in a dead slouch. It is evergreen, still alive in this cold terrain, as if to inform explorers that things can and will survive here.

♦♦♦

I stopped at a ratty gas station along the way and got gas and pork rinds. I never had pork rinds, and that's why I got them. I don't know. I felt strange doing this, going out to see my dad, so I bought pork rinds.

They were horrible. They smelled like a big man's armpit and rotten potato chips, if potato chips could get rotten.

♦♦♦

I double-checked I didn't have even a trace of weed on me before I went in. Went through the metal detectors. Innocent as a choir boy. There were plenty of visitors there with me—wives and children bundled up nicely in their fat coats. Their faces were sad or expressionless. The wives, I mean. Most of the children were hootin' and hollerin' or cryin' their fuckin' eyes out for no apparent reason. Children made me sweat.

I was escorted to a room that looked like a small cafeteria. Every surface was hard and sterile and bolted down. The lights hummed above us. I sat at an empty table and waited, cracking my knuckles again and again even though they weren't cracking anymore.

He had a beard and a shaved head when he appeared, but I still recognized him. I was tempted to look away when we saw each other, but instead, I smiled politely. He didn't smile. But it wasn't like an unfriendly or intimidating lack of a smile. More like a face when you've forgotten how to socialize. I don't know. That's what he did.

"You look like me," he said.

"Yeah, well, of course," I said. Not in a rude way, mind you. A poor joke way. An awkward way.

"It's been a while," he said.

"Yeah. You come here often?" I get particularly not funny when I'm nervous. I don't know.

"Ha," he said, finally smiling a little.

The strange part about sitting right in front of each other like that is you never know where to look. You can't just stare right into each other's eyes the whole time but looking down makes you look somber and whatnot. There's nothing interesting to see elsewhere. Inmates and their families have the exact same struggle: a soulless prison hog and tile. That's it.

He went, "So, what have you been up to? You in school?"

"I dropped out."

"Are you serious?"

"Yeah."

"Come on, man, why?"

"I don't know. I make too much money at my job, so why would I bother getting into debt?"

"Yeah, your job. Got it."

I looked up at him, not knowing how to respond.

"Yeah, your mother told me in a letter," he said.

I got bold and said, "Well, you're hardly in a position to criticize."

"I'm in the perfect position to criticize. You want to end up like me or somethin'?"

"No."

"Well."

One of the correctional hogs started maddoggin' us. So, I started whispering like, "It's just weed."

"That's where it starts."

"Nah, that's all.

He leaned back in his chair, all doubtful-like, saying, "Okay."

We were silent again, looking for things to look at. Across the way, a woman was crying, and the inmate across from her was trying to calm her. There was a little play area for kids with, like, four picture books that lay there scrunched on their pages. Some broken toys, too. None of the kids were using them.

My dad put his elbows onto the table and said, "Yeah maybe you're right. I can't criticize anyone. I was selling blow to get my way through grad school."

"Grad school?" I asked. This motherfucker never went to grad school, as far as I knew. Murderers don't go to grad school.

"Yeah, man. I'm Doctor Washburn."

"What?"

"Yeah," he said, all casual-like.

"You have a Ph.D.?"

"Yeah."

"In what?"

"English literature. Your mother never told you that?"

"No," I said. I wasn't sure if he was telling the truth or not. Maybe all that time in his cell made him genuinely think he had a Ph.D. Like self-proclaimed or some shit. Reading every waking hour.

So, I was all like, "From where?"

"UB," he said. "I get your disbelief. It's strange to me, too. Academia is a horrible place, though. Education isn't. Besides health and happiness, that's the most important thing in this world. Academia doesn't give a shit about education, though. It gives a shit about itself. I liked to write. I liked to read. I liked the bikes. I liked to get high. You know. It all went the wrong way. Tom Wolfe's got a Ph.D."

"Oh yeah. I think I heard that," I said, as if I knew who Tom Wolfe was.

"You do much reading, Bobby?"

"Yeah. Here and there."

"Good, man."

I told him I liked Cormac McCarthy. I didn't know this at the time, but Cormac McCarthy dropped out of college, too. He didn't tell me that, though. I bet you he knew that, but he didn't tell me. He gave me a beautiful lecture on Blood Meridian instead. Most of what he said blew over my head except when he was all like, "A lot of readers probably find Judge Holden unrealistic. I encourage them to meet some of my colleagues in here."

We started talking about the weather, as you do when you don't know what else to talk about.

He said, "In here, we all prefer the winter. It's summer when it gets brutal. The AC always breaks, and they take their damn time to fix it."

"I hate it," I said. "I wanna move down south."

"I had the same notion when I was around your age. But Buffalo has a way of calling you back. I don't know why. It just does."

Silence again between us. Controlled eye movement.

"You got any prison tattoos?" I asked.

"No," he said, unamused.

Right back to the fuckin' silence again. Humans weren't made to do things like this. Prison visits were never in God's plan. I was sure of it. My dad must've been used to it or something because he seemed sweatless the whole time.

"Washburn," the hog said. "Five minutes."

I got all nervous, so I said, "How's the food in here?"

"Not particularly great. You get used to it."

"You ever have pork rinds?"

"What?"

"Pork rinds. You know what those are?"

"I hate pork rinds. They smell weird."

I laughed and said, "I know!"

"Why? Someone got pork rinds?" He looked around.

"No, I just tried them on the ride here because I'd never had them before."

"Oh, yeah, they're horrible."

"Horrible."

"Some of the guys in the club liked them a lot."

I laughed again. "Yeah, I can see bikers liking pork rinds."

He laughed, too. "Yeah," he said. "Bikers and truckers are

probably the sole demographic across the world who enjoy pork rinds."

"So, if I sent you some pork rinds in here, would you eat them?"

He sat back in mediation. "Now that's a challenging question. I do get particularly bored in here. But still, probably not. Anything else, yes."

"You could trade them for a shank."

He laughed. "I'm not that good at bartering, Bobby."

The hogs approached us and started breathing all down my dad's neck. They were all like, "Times up, Washburn."

My dad stood. He was tall and strong. He towered over me and them, too. Orange jumpsuit. Hard and battered arms. He said, "I'd shake your hand, but they don't let us touch."

"Ah," I said.

He gave me a downward nod. "It was good to see you, Bobby."

"You too," I said.

"All right then," he said, then turned and left.

I hadn't noticed his shoes until then. They looked like cheap slippers. They were pathetic. Pathetic slippers on this monstrous, brilliant man.

♦♦♦

The holidays were a good time for drug dealers. Folks are more prone to treat themselves. Or they're having a last hurrah before they quit smoking for their New Year's Resolution. Though they always come crawling back. Certainly.

I was out and about selling. Twitchy Walter hit my lick, asking to meet at Ruby Tuesday. I don't know why this motherfucker was always wandering around the most random parts of town, but he was. I stopped questioning it. At least he saved my number this time.

On my way, I texted.

Ruby Tuesday wasn't too far away, but the traffic was shit as it always is around Christmas time. I contemplated if I should get a gift for Gerald or not. I hadn't gotten one for any of Ma's boyfriends in the past, but this one had stuck around the longest. I didn't know what his hobbies were, nor did I really care. It was probably birdwatching or building model airplanes or something dorky like that.

I pulled into the turning lane and waited for the path to clear. Salty cars with black snow caked to their tire frames went by on the slippery road. A slushy sound.

I parked in a space but didn't see Walter anywhere. I called him, and he was like, "Hello?"

"I'm here," I said.

"Where are you?"

"Here. In the parking lot."

"I don't see you. What kind of car are you in?"

"A white Nissan."

"I don't see you."

"Well, I'm here, bro."

"Which Arby's are you at?"

"Arby's?"

"Yeah."

"Motherfucker you said Ruby Tuesday."

"Oh," he said, all dopey-like. "Oh. I always get those mixed up."

"What? How?"

"I don't know."

"Are you high?"

"Yeah."

"Jesus Christ."

So, sure enough, Walter's twitchy ass was standing outside of the Arby's by the mall. I pulled up, and he got right in all mechanical-like.

He looked at me, expressionless, as if he were a fuckin' corpse, and said, "Hi, Bobby."

I was all like, "Hi."

"That's a cool Funko Pop," he said, even though his tone said otherwise. I didn't know what the fuck that was. I had a bobblehead of Andre the Giant. That's what I always called them.

"Thanks," I said. "You all right?"

"Yes. I'm fine."

"How much did you smoke?"

"I didn't."

"I thought you said you were high."

"I am."

"On what then?"

"Xanax."

It was then that I noticed that Walter wasn't twitchy. I had fucked around with benzos in the past. To me, the high felt like being drunk without the mental buzz of being drunk, so I'd rather just be drunk. But the shit seemed to work wonders on Walter. This zombie-like state was actually a lot less alarming than his typical skittishness.

"So did your therapist prescribe you that or some shit?" I asked.

"What?" he said. "No. I bought it."

"Oh damn. Who's the Xanax plug?"

"The dark web."

I had heard of the dark web and all its varieties. It was the sector of the Internet where you could buy illegal shit. All the way from crack to straps.

"You know how to get to that?" I asked.

"Yeah," he said.

"Is it safe?"

"Yeah."

I gave him an eight. He paid me forty, though he still owed me more from the last two. I reminded him of that. He said he'd get it to me soon, as they always say.

Before he ventured back out to the snow, he said, "That's a cool Funko Pop."

"Yeah, you mentioned that."

"What?"

"Forget it."

♦♦♦

It was Christmas Eve. Ma started going on about how we should go to Midnight Mass up at Saint Louis. I fuckin' hated Midnight Mass. She was all like, "Bobby, you wear a gold crucifix, but you never go to church anymore. Kind of fake, don't you think?"

She knew how to get to me.

She was all like, "Bobby, you sell drugs. It'd probably be in your best interest to make peace with God."

"I sell weed, Ma."

"Do you think Jesus would approve?"

Saint Louis was the tallest church in Buffalo. Probably the oldest, too—or at least one of the oldest. Its interior was cavernous and spectacular with tall stained-glass windows telling stories of early martyrs and disciples. Barely clothed Nazarites with their heads dangling, their bodies spiked with Roman arrows and Roman pikes. Cloaked women with their hands in prayer and their eyes to the sky. The Messiah healing demoniacs and lepers with the touch of a carpenter's callused hand.

I dipped my sinful fingers in the font and did the sign of the cross, wetting my forehead just a bit. Gerald dipped his hand in and just touched his forehead because he saw me do it. I don't think Gerald was much of a church-going guy either. Shit still stays with me, though, no matter how much I sin.

Ma was now obnoxiously drunk. She said, "Bobby, let's sit in the front! We never sit in the front!"

"All right, Ma. Quiet down."

"What? What?"

I followed Ma to the front pew. She tried to genuflect but lost her balance and fell backward onto her butt. She was all like, "Whoops!"

The whole fuckin' flock was looking at us. I mouthed, *Sorry*, then genuflected myself and sat beside her. Gerald tried to genuflect but just sort of tea-bagged the floor. Poor guy. He really tried.

Ma whispered to me, "Bobby."

"What?"

"My butt's wet."

She'd fallen into a puddle that formed from the snow melting off everyone's shoes.

"We can leave," I said.

"No, no, no. I'm fine. I'm fine. Bobby, I'm fine."

"Okay, Jesus Christ."

"Hey!"

I looked behind me. The church was piling full of patrons, and it felt like they were all looking at us. I don't know whose brilliant idea Midnight Mass was, or why we still agreed to do it, but we did. Everyone looked more tired and miserable than they usually did at church, and people at church often look really tired and miserable—unless they're into it. But those are few and far between nowadays, I think. I don't know. Maybe I'm just projecting. Probably.

So, one of the deacons approached the altar. He gave us his little deacon-like spiel, thanking us for congregating to the house of God or whatever. The priest was an Italian guy, Father Tony, flanked by two altar boys all fresh out of Sunday School. Back in the day, I chose Homobonus as my confirmation name. Primarily because I was a smartass, but also because Saint Homobonus is the patron saint of businessmen. I knew that I wanted to sling drugs, even back then.

Father Tony came to the altar and said softly into the microphone, "Let us pray," and we all stood. There were hundreds of us in the church. I eyed Ma's butt, and it was indeed soaked. The priest told us to look around and greet one another, as they always do. Ma started shaking everyone's hand saying, "Peace be with you. Peace be with you."

"Ma," I whispered.

"Peace be with you! Peace be with you, ma'am. Ma'am. Ma'am. Peace be with you."

"Ma."

"What, Bobby?"

"We do that later."

In Catholic Mass, you first greet one another with a wave, then halfway through you shake hands and say, "Peace be with you." Ma mixed these up.

She was all like, "Bobby, I think I would know."

"Then why are you the only one doing it?"

She looked around.

"We do that later, Ma."

"Oh," she said.

Every part of me regretted coming. I shouldn't have let her talk me into it. And who knew how much longer we had to go? These holiday Masses were always long as fuck.

Whenever Father Tony said, "Peace be with you," Ma was all like, "And also with you!" even though the entire fuckin' church was saying, "And with your spirit."

The response used to be, "And also with you," but they changed it to, "And with your spirit," a few years back. Every time she did it, she said, "Whoops!" as if it were her first time doing it.

"Why does she keep saying that?" whispered Gerald.

"I'll explain later," I sighed.

Saint Louis had these elephantine organ pipes in the balcony, and they started humming like some cataclysmic wind. They were beautiful. Everyone got their books and started singing along with the choir. I saw Ma reach for the book in the pew slot so I snatched it before she could. "No," I said.

"Bobby, give me the book."

"No."

She maddoged me for a second then grabbed the book and started fighting me for it, smacking at my arms and tugging and whatnot, making a fuckin' spectacle. I let her have it just so she would stop.

She rifled through the book and was all like, "What page was it?"

I didn't say anything.

The voice of the choir was behind us. "O come, O come, Emmaa-Aaa-Aaa-nuel."

"Bobby, what page was it?"

"I don't know."

She put the book down and hollered, "RE-JOOOOICE, RE-JOOOOICE, EMM-aaa-AAA-aa-AANU-EL! SHALL COME TO YOU, O Iii-Iii-IS-RAEL!"

Father Tony looked over. Guess we were all going to hell.

Eventually, the deacon and some other volunteers went to the tabernacle to get the bread and wine. *Thank fuckin' God*, I was thinking—no pun intended. If there was anything I learned from my Catholic upbringing, it was that when you ate the sacrament, that meant Mass was almost over.

When they were ready, the other people in the front row started heading toward the aisle.

"Should I go?" asked Gerald.

"Yeah," I said.

"Don't you need to be, like, official or something to get the wafer?"

"Yeah, but nobody cares."

"Are you sure?"

"Yes. How would they know?"

Gerald looked to the aisle with hesitation. "I don't think I should go," he said.

"Oh my God," Ma said all sacrilegious. "Then get out of the way,"

I got in line, and Ma came up behind me. I heard her giggling and whatnot, but I just ignored it. *Just a few more minutes*, I told myself. Just a few more minutes, then I'd never come to church again. Yes. Absolutely. I was officially an atheist from here on out. Denounce Homobonus and all. No God would do this to someone.

We slowly wobbled forward like penguins, but the extra help made it go fast. I squared up with Father Tony. He looked at me with eyes of pity, or maybe he was just tired since it was, like, almost 1 AM.

He said, "The body of Christ."

I said, "Amen," then he handed me the wafer. The body of Christ. He tasted like cardboard. I skipped the wine, as everyone did. Then I realized something. Who was the one Catholic in this church who'd certainly want a taste of the alcoholic blood of Christ? I looked behind me, and Ma was making her way to the unlucky bastard with the wine. She took the chalice and drank more than a sip. She went to give it back but stopped herself. "Just one more sip," she said, then drank again.

The deacon coughed.

After a third sip, Ma gave it back, then turned to the entire church. Some madness came upon her, and she rose both arms, and said, "WOOOOOOOOO! I GOT THE BLOOD OF JESUS CHRIST IN MY BELLY TONIGHT!"

Everything, and everyone, became silent and motionless. I thought I was hallucinating. Father Tony had finally lost his patience, waving his hand to signal a few men in suits to pull her out. I was already back at my pew grabbing all our coats when Father Tony took one last look at me. He said with his eyes, "Get this bitch out of my church."

♦♦♦

In the car, she said, "What? Oh my God, it was just some fun. Nobody can take a joke anymore."

Then she vomited all over herself.

She said, "Whoops!"

♦♦♦

Christmas morning was just me and Gerald because Ma was so hungover in bed. We listened to her scream into the toilet bowl as we sipped our coffee.

I ended up getting him two bobbleheads for his car. It was those two grouchy old Muppets—the two who are always talking shit from above.

"I get a lot of compliments on my Andre the Giant bobblehead, so I figured I'd get you some," I said.

"I love it," he said, and he sounded like he meant it. He held them and gazed at them all lovestruck-like.

"Here," he said, handing me the gift he got for me.

It was actually wrapped quite well and in the recognizable square shape of a CD. I should mention I didn't wrap mine. Ma and I stopped doing that years ago.

I tore it open to find one of Gucci Mane's albums.

"Gucci Mane. Huh," I said.

"Yeah. Isn't that what all the kids are listening to?" he asked.

"Yeah, yeah. Thanks, Gerald."

I hadn't used a CD since I was, like, eleven years old, nor did I really care for Gucci Mane. I wasn't gonna tell him that, though. It was a kind gesture. It really was.

"Bur," said Gerald.

He made some gesture with his hand I didn't get. Probably something Gucci Mane did in music videos.

"Yes," I said, "Bur."

♦♦♦

Now it was my turn to get fucked up, so I went over to Frank's in the afternoon. The only day of the year I actually enjoyed snow was Christmas Day. I didn't know how those fuckin' southerners celebrated Christmas without snow. What'd they tell their kids? That Santa wore a fuckin' Speedo? This was really just the envy speaking. I envied their weather more than anything. Humans weren't made to live in Buffalo. I'll never stop saying that.

But anyway, they can envy our white Christmases. I liked when there was fresh snow on Christmas Day. I admired the waves of it on everyone's lawn as I drove through the quiet suburbs. Comfort and joy, as they say. Good tidings and shit.

I got bold and just walked into Frank's without texting him first. I knew his parents weren't gonna say anything about it. They were probably scared of me, too. Salt and Pepper, those fuckin' schnauzers, started nippin' at my knees.

I was all like, "Get. Get!"

Frank's dad appeared in a Santa hat, and he was like, "Salt, Pepper, come here," all monotone and shit. They listened, though, surprisingly. If I were their dog, I'd do whatever the fuck I wanted.

"Hi," I said to the dad. "Merry Christmas."

"Merry Christmas," he said.

The mom appeared, same expressionless face. "Merry Christmas," she said.

"Is Frank upstairs?" I asked.

"Yes. With one of his friends."

"Huh, all right," I said all confused.

I went upstairs and opened Frank's door to see him leaning over some kid's shoulder at the laptop. I stepped in and realized it was fuckin' Walter. Fuckin' twitchy bike tire Walter. What the hell was he doing here?

Frank saw me and said, "Yo."

I said, "Uh, yo."

"Hi, Bobby," said Walter, all barred out.

"What are you guys doing?" I asked.

"Buying Xanax off the dark web," said Walter.

I looked at Frank, and he looked at me, excitement in his smile. Finally, he had something to be happy about. But I felt like this was probably just the beginning of something very worrying.

He said, "We're making a new business venture, Bobby."

Walter clicked the mouse a few times. Frank rustled his shoulders, like a boxer's coach after getting a knockdown.

"Merry fuckin' Christmas," Frank said.

II.

Look, there was no morality behind it. This wasn't a question of right from wrong. Life just moved the way it did, and I never had any say. Okay? I wasn't a bad person.

Xanax was the Quaalude of the 2000s. For a while, shrinks were handing that shit out like it was Aspirin. And pretty much everyone in America claimed to have an anxiety disorder. They probably did, actually. How could you not? So, a lot of people got hooked on the stuff.

Thing was, like any drug, you build a tolerance pretty quickly. And, suddenly, the doctor's prescription isn't enough to cut it. This was at the dawn of the dark web. The Internet was getting so big that everyone carried it around in their pocket. Skinny white boys who got teased in high school started learning how to slither their way into the dark underworld of this virtual universe—started doing some sinister shit. Drug dealers came to see it as a new market. Websites like the Silk Road formed as a hub for all illegal transactions. Now any thirteen-year-old punk who knew his way around the Internet could have a kilo of cocaine and a MAC-10 delivered right to his doorstep. The glory of it was that the hogs didn't know how to stop it. They were still asking their kids how to "email a Facebook."

Xanax was one of the bestsellers on the dark web. You could buy thousands of them. Now, technically, they weren't *real* Xanax. They weren't made by whatever company makes it. Xanax is the chemical alprazolam. It's in the benzodiazepine family—often shortened to benzos. Drug dealers would buy alprazolam powder from, like, Sri Lanka, or some shit, then make their pill presses to form tablets that resembled Xanax. So, it was essentially the same as the real thing, though sometimes they'd cut it with other shit, I'm sure.

Frank realized he could make a hell of a lot more money selling Xanax than weed. Street value was $5 a 2 mg bar. They're shaped like rectangles. Kinda look like mints. We would each buy 1,000 bars for $1,000. That's a $4,000 profit, and that shit sold *quick*. Some of our most loyal clients bought twenty bars a day.

It wasn't long before the three of us were all out of our parents' house. Yeah, Walter was in the crew now. As weird as that sounds, we needed him to work the web.

We'd buy it off the same connect so many times that they knew to pack them into separate bags. The connect on Silk Road was called XanRunner96. Naturally, we knew nothing about the guy. Might not have even been a guy, as far as we knew.

Shit changed after that first bag. I was in the Big Leagues of drug dealing as they say.

I'll say it again: There was no morality behind it. It just happened.

Of course, I feel guilty now. Why do you think I'm writing this?

♦♦♦

Frank rented a house out in North Buffalo. I had a studio apartment elsewhere, but his house was basically my third home. He started depositing some dealing funds into a checking account to make it look like he was an honest, blue-collar man. Paid rent in cashier checks from the local deli. The landlord never batted an eyelash, according to him. It was nice though, and incognito shit is what three young punks needed to blend in.

Our mailman was Craig. I don't know if Craig knew what we

were up to, but he certainly found it bizarre. Three young men anxiously wait for the same package every week. We could've been more secretive about it—rotate addresses, not greet the mailman—but we had become far too cocky.

It was summer then, after what felt like the longest winter of my life. Buffalo doesn't really have a spring. It's just a slushier, slightly-less-cold winter. It does get hot in the summer, though, and that day was certainly hot. Shooting the shit, just drinking beer and smoking cigarettes. Didn't matter what day it was. Every day is the weekend when you're a drug dealer. It was a flexible career path. No health insurance, though. But health insurance was the last thing on our minds. As I said, very cocky.

We would wait for the mailman like we were old widows waiting for their ghostly husbands. We tormented the guy. That day he came huffing down the street in his mailman clothes. He was a bulky and hairy man. Sweaty. Very sweaty on days such as this one.

Frank stood and was all like, "There he is! The man of the hour!"

Craig smiled all bashful-like.

He put envelopes in the neighbors' mailboxes and huffed over to us.

"Craig," I said with a gentleman's nod.

"Hey guys," he said. He came up the creaky steps, that familiar package in hand. "Here ya go."

I took hold of the package.

"You always come through right when we need you, Craig," said Frank, smiling all shitty-like.

"Yeah," he said all nervous-like, "Ha-ha."

"You want a beer, Craig?" I asked.

"No. Well. I can't. I would. What is that?" He examined the beer.

"Labatt," I said.

"Oh, cool. I like Labatt."

"Have one, Craig," said Frank. "You've earned it."

"Well," he said, "On the clock. I gotta get goin', guys."

"All right, Craig. Good to see ya."

"Take it easy, Craig."

"Bye, Craig," said Walter, all barred out, nearly a whisper.

That kid was a fiend now. I guess he had a better excuse than others. Frank took the package from me and started ripping it open right in broad daylight. Fearless.

They were about the size of your standard lunch baggie, though packed rather fat. I loved the feeling of it. I explored the little pills with my fingertips. I took a good pull of my beer, a few thick drags of the cigarette, then crushed it into the ashtray, letting the smoke pour up my hand.

"I guess I should get to work now," I said.

♦♦♦

Back in the weed days, fronting was good for business. That changed come the Xanax days. We were the *only* kingpins. Any other Xanax dealer in Buffalo got his shit from us. So, with that being the new situation, there was no need to front. Reputation meant nothing. We had a fuckin' monopoly on the market. If you didn't like our practices, well, then no Xanax for you. It was wonderful.

I had a bunch of clients to see that day. It always worked like that when we re-upped. I tried to prioritize by quantity. This kid named Kyle was one of the dealers beneath me, so I went to his place first.

I drove over there. His apartment door wasn't ajar—it was wide open. I stepped in there all like, "Uh, yo?"

The room was hot and vile. There were beer cans everywhere. The floor was caked in shoe prints. The dishes were yea high and covered in generations and generations of fruit flies. Upstairs, I found Kyle asleep on the floor beside his bed. I wasn't sure if he didn't make it in or if he rolled off at some point.

I shook him gently and his eyes shot awake. He started freaking out, all like, "WHAT? WHAT? WHAT?"

I was all like, "Woah, dude. Relax."

He came to his senses and said, "Aw shit. Sorry, Bobby. How you doin'?"

"How are *you* doin'? D'you fall out of bed?"

He looked at his bed beside him as if he'd only just noticed that he wasn't in it. "Oh," he said. "Yeah, apparently."

"I got your shit," I said, pulling out the hundred bars.

"What shit?"

"You high, Kyle?"

"Well, yeah. A little still."

"You wanted a hundred bars."

"Oh. Right. Gimme a sec."

I saw where this was going. "You got the money, right?" I asked.

"Yeah, yeah, yeah, definitely. Lemme see where I put it."

I knew what that meant. I wasn't leaving with my money.

Fuckhead Kyle started digging through his dresser drawers which were stuffed with various papers and receipts and shit like that. He abandoned the drawer, leaving it open. It was about to fall from the rest of the dresser. He went to the pairs of grimy pants scattered across the floor and dug through their pockets. He was all like, "Where the fuck is my wallet, bro?"

Finally, he went to his little safe and found the wallet and the wad of twenties and he paid me. I wasn't expecting that. It was going to be a good day.

◆◆◆

My next client was a doctor. Isn't that ironic? Apparently, doctors can't prescribe themselves Xannies. I think he was actually in his residency or something like that. I don't know. He was sometimes still in his white doctor's coat when I went over to the hospital. He was waiting for me in a Lexus. Guess he was getting the one-up on the high life.

I said, "What's up?"

And he said, "Hey, how do you do?"

He was, like, twenty-nine, and already balding. That doctor life must've been stressful. I was curious what kind of doctor he was. If he was a urologist or some shit like that, then I guess being a bar-head wouldn't be so bad. But if he was a surgeon and under the spell of alprazolam, he'd certainly cut the wrong vein or fall asleep with his hands in someone's guts. I didn't ask, though.

He was buying ten pills or something like that. I gave him the bag, and he gave me exact change, like always. Most people paid in twenties for our bars. Doctor Balding, though, gave me fives. I liked him for that.

◆◆◆

I still visited my mom. Every Sunday, I went over there for dinner. Gerald had moved in at that point, though they were still as weirdly distant as they always were. I don't know. I don't know what the hell he saw in her. He could've probably done better than her. Maybe not. Yeah, probably not actually.

I stepped inside the house and the fuckin' bird swooped down from its perch and tried to claw my eye out. I dodged it and swatted. It flew back to its perch and sat there glaring, all contemptuous-like. Its bird eyes were saying, "Yeah, this is my house, punk." Ma got drunk one day and wandered to the pet store and bought a fuckin' bird. A cockatiel, I think they're called. The fucker was mean as shit and hated me in particular. Gerald was scared of it, too. He was hiding around the corner, all like, "Did it go back to its perch?"

"Yeah," I said. "It almost clawed me."

"Don't make eye contact with it. That makes it attack." He was completely serious, too.

"What are you making tonight?" I asked.

"Pork chops."

"Word. Where's Ma at?"

"She's in the back."

Ma was lying on a beach chair, but the beach before her was an uncut backyard. It was tall enough to hold coyotes. She had on the big-ass sunglasses that made her look like a bug, and she was smoking a bowl. When she saw me, she said, "Oh, hi honey."

I got closer and realized it wasn't weed in there. It was some red and black chunky liquid.

"Ma, what are you smoking?"

"Advil," she said.

I was speechless for a moment. She held the lighter flame and melted the pills and inhaled. She coughed viciously, spitting it all out.

"Why the fuck are you smoking Advil?"

She looked at me as if that were a stupid question. "I can't swallow the pills, Bobby. You know that."

"That doesn't mean you smoke it. You can't smoke Advil, Ma."

"It goes straight to the brain," she said, then lifted the bowl to her lips once again.

I grabbed it from her. "Ma, stop."

"What? Bobby, I have a SPLITTING headache."

"I'll buy you some drinkable medicine."

She contemplated that. "Oh, no, no. I don't enjoy the taste." She lifted a White Trash Mimosa from beside her and took a sip.

"Ma, if ten cocktails aren't helping your headache, I don't think Advil will. Why don't you drink some water? You're probably dehydrated."

"I drink plenty of water," she said.

"I don't think I've ever seen you drink water once in my life."

"Stop," she said, all deflective-like, taking a hit of the White Trash Mimosa.

I went to the side door and entered the garage. They had a fridge out there designated for beers and Gerald's Mike's Hard Lemonades. The aesthetic of a fridge full of nothing but colorful cans and bottles was pleasing. I twisted the cap off a Labatt, chugged it like a frat boy, then tossed the bottle into a pile of clutter. Fuck it.

♦♦♦

I had thrown back like three or four more while waiting for the food. The older I got, the more I understood why adults threw 'em back after every workday and weekend. How could you not? But, even with the alcohol, that fuckin' bird still made me nervous.

The pork chops were very Bob-Evans-esque. So overcooked, but edible. They tasted like salt. I was too hard on Gerald. The guy could cook a hell of a lot better than I could. Those Sundays were actually the only homecooked meal I had. I never cooked for myself. Once I had enough money to constantly get delivery, I did.

We ate in silence for some moments. That fuckin' bird was watching me, all sentinel-like. It was calmer when Ma was in the room. It swooped down and landed on her shoulder. Ma was all like, "Hi, Catherine. Oh, you want some pork chop, Catherine? You want some porky porky? You want some pork pork?" She tried to feed the bird a little sliver of meat, but it just pecked at it. "Fine, fine, sorry," Ma said.

I said, "Thank you for dinner, Gerald."

"You're welcome," he said.

That motherfucker always said, "You're welcome." It was never no problem or of course with him. Guess it was ingrained from the ethos or whatever.

"Yes, thank you, dear," said Ma.

"You're welcome. Try it with the applesauce."

He provided little bowls of applesauce beside each entree. It was cute.

"Catherine doesn't like it, though," said Ma.

I could tell Gerald was annoyed by that comment, but he didn't dare say anything disrespectful to Catherine. She was to be feared and respected.

◆◆◆

I stayed over, so I just kept drinking the 12-pack. I had some clients stop by. We met by the side door and did the business in the garage.

I went back inside, and Ma was all like, "Bobby, if you're gonna sell out of my house, I expect some commission."

That was fair. I gave her fifty bucks.

We were in the living room, watching TV and drinking. Ma looked at my new gold watch and said, "I want the luxury life, Bobby."

"Yeah?"

"I want to suck caviar right out of the fish's cunt."

"What the fuck, Ma?"

Then Gerald from the other room was all like, "Ay, woah, ay, don't talk to your mother like that."

"Did you hear what she said?"

Ma was all like, "Bobby, what I'm saying is that I want in on the action."

"What?" I asked.

"I want to sell dope."

I got all prideful-like. "Nah, Ma. It's not for you."

"No, Bobby. It is."

"Are you having trouble with money?"

She motioned her hands to imply I should see the room around us. "Look. Look, Bobby. Does all this look satisfactory to you?"

I looked. "Yeah," I said.

"No, Bobby. I want *more*. Your father promised me *more,* and he couldn't do it. So now you must. No, no. Now *I* must. I want in."

She was pointing her pointer finger all drunk-like.

Gerald walked in. "What's goin' on in here?"

Ma said, "And *this* man ain't doin' nothing either."

Gerald looked at me. "Bobby, what's she going on about?"

"I don't even know, man."

"Carol, what are you going on about?"

A terrible rage came upon her. She went to stand but struggled and fell back onto the couch. "I'm not happy with this life," she said. "You think this was how I saw myself when I was a little girl?"

She started to cry. She buried her head into her legs and hollered sobs. Her blind hand reached for the White Trash Mimosa and spilled it onto the coffee table. "Oh, fuck," she said. "Look at this. This is me." The orange liquid spread to the edge of the table and began to drip into the rug.

Gerald and I looked at each other, not knowing how to react. Then he said, "Uh, I'll go get some paper towels."

He left me alone with my wailing mother. I thought the boyfriend was supposed to be the one to comfort. Ma cried plenty, but it was usually over some stupid shit like Gerald picking up the wrong pack of cigarettes or something. Never deep shit like this.

I stood up and walked over to her all stiff-like. I sat beside her. Her wails had turned into a sloppy whimper. I guessed I was supposed to put my arm around her, so I did. It felt weird.

I was all like, "Uh, it's all right, Ma."

I don't think I convinced her. She kept on whimpering. Gerald returned with the paper towels and cleaned up the mess. We just sat there, me and Ma, until she fell asleep five minutes later.

◆◆◆

So, Ma took another stab at sobriety that morning. She was all done up, makeup and everything. She said, "I'm going to church, Bobby. It would do you well to come, too."

"Which church?" I asked.

She looked at me all annoyed-like. "Not that one," she said. "I'll go to Saint Chris's."

"I've got too much shit to do today," I said.

"Fine," she said. "I'm not going to pass judgment on you." Even though she was clearly passing judgment on me.

She left and got in Gerald's truck. I was pretty confident that she had never driven a truck before, but there was no stopping her once she made up her mind.

Something strange came upon me. I had an urge to get incredibly drunk, right there, at 10 in the morning, or however early it was. Certainly, it was before noon. I actually would hardly call it an urge. It was more just an action that came upon me. A spirit. I poured a shot of vodka and threw it back. Blah. Buh. Hew.

I went to the garage and got a beer. Cracked it. Drank. Ah.

I went to the kitchen and lit a cigarette. Gerald came down in his Bob Evans uniform. He didn't have anything to say about my morning drinking. He must've been used to it. He poured coffee into his Thermos. He had that grouchy, sleepy face that people have in the morning. Suddenly that face shot awake when he looked out the window. "Where's my truck?" he asked.

"Oh," I said, exhaling smoke. "Ma took it."

"Are you fucking kidding me?"

Gerald didn't swear often.

"I figured she asked you."

"No, she didn't ask me!"

"Well don't get mad at me, man."

He let out a frustrated groan. "Where'd she go?"

"Church."

"Are you serious?"

"Yeah, Saint Chris's"

"Oh my God."

I let him borrow my car while I just kicked back and drank, drank, drank. The bird was hollerin' like a motherfucker. I avoided it and just turned the TV on to *The Price is Right*.

♦♦♦

So, it was pretty light that day on the dealing side of things. There never seemed to be any rhyme or reason for it. People quit and relapsed a lot.

I was chilling. The TV was still on, but I wasn't watching it. After the last customer, I chained smoked. I was just letting the smoke float from my mouth in meditation.

My phone started buzzing. I sat up all perturbed-like and checked it. It was Nora. Nora was calling me. Frank's girl.

I crushed the cig and cleared my throat, preparing.

"Hello?" I said.

"Yo," she said.

"What's up?"

"You around right now?"

"Yeah."

"Could I get some bars off you right now? I don't know where Frank's at."

"Of course. I'm at my Ma's. You know where that is?"

"Uh, nah, give me directions?"

A lot of people feel less anxiety when they drink. I feel just as much, if not more sometimes. I don't know. I was nervous. Maybe it just depended on the situation. But right then, as drunk as I was, I was nervous.

She came quite quickly. I put the TV on mute. I heard her car pull up and stop. A door closed. I heard her gentle footsteps.

When she came, I was all like, "Yo, what's up?"

And she was all like, "Yo."

She was dressed casually. White short shorts. A ponytail.

"Decent place."

"Yeah. I'm home alone, though. I mean, they wouldn't care otherwise."

"Could I just get, like, two bars?"

"Of course, of course," I said.

She came in and saw the bird cage.

"Whoa, is this a bird?"

I turned around to get the big bag of pills hiding beside the couch.

"You don't wanna see that bitch," I said.

She didn't listen. Catherine was unusually calm. Maybe she felt safe for once.

"Aw, it's so cute," Nora said. "Can I hold it?"

I started pinching out the pills, making sure I gave her a bit more. "Nah, I wouldn't do that."

She didn't listen. In the few seconds it took Nora to reach toward the bird, Catherine pounced. I heard the horrible swoop and flap of wings. The death-squawks. I knew at once what was about to happen.

Catherine, the demon bird, took hold of Nora's ponytail and

started pecking and pulling like an endless worm buffet. Nora was screaming and swatting at it. The bird got its talons stuck in her hair and was sparring with Nora's hand.

I ran over there trying to help, going, "Oh shit, oh shit, sorry, oh my God, sorry, hold still, oh my God, shit, hold still, hold still."

"Get it out!" she hollered.

I got ahold of the bird and pulled at it, but its foot was still tangled in Nora's hair. The bird's scream changed to the high-pitched *reep reep reep,* then it dug its fuckin' beak right into my finger and squeezed.

Now I was fuckin' screaming, too.

Somehow, in the fit of swatting, the bird came loose and flew back to its perch. Nora ran for cover behind the couch, and I followed. We were both panting for air.

She asked, "What the fuck, Bobby?"

"Sorry," I said. "She just...I don't know. She just does that sometimes."

"She just does that sometimes?"

Figures, the one time I get a girl over, that shit happened.

I ended up giving her ten pills on the house and some old band-aids. She wasn't happy. My stomach hurt the rest of the day.

◆◆◆

Ma came home hours later and looked at me on the couch. She was all serious-like. "I meant what I said, Bobby. I'm ashamed of myself. I'm big enough to admit that I'm powerless over alcohol."

I kind of just nodded my head. I was drunk and still nursing my bird bite. Catherine slept on her perch, seemingly an angel.

"And if I'm being honest, Bobby, I think you should consider admitting the same. I see me in you."

I was all like, "What do you mean?"

"I think you're an alcoholic, Bobby. You're drunk right now."

"Don't turn this around on me."

"I'm not turning this around on you. I think we should get sober together."

I was all slurry and shit, saying stuff like, "Who the fuck are you to judge me?"

"I'm not."

"No, you *are*. You always have to take the blame off yourself somehow. This isn't a group effort. You're the fuck up. Not me."

She walked away all smug-like, and just said, "Sad."

I almost said nothing. For a moment I said nothing, but then I said, "Fuck you."

She turned slowly. "What did you just say to me?"

"You heard."

"Get out of my house."

"I would if Gerald didn't have my car."

"Why does Gerald have your car?"

"Because you took his."

"Oh. Well, when he gets back, you get out."

"Gladly."

"And don't come back."

"Gladly."

♦♦♦

Gerald came back in a good mood. He was like, "Hey, Bobby!" And I just said, "Give me my keys."

He said, "Oh, okay, sure," and complied.

I drove home. Still drunk. And mad, and slightly horny. The unholy trifecta.

♦♦♦

The next day, I was stopping at this motherfucker named Roy's house. He was an aspiring UFC fighter. He'd fought in plenty of lower-level fights, trying to work his way up the ladder. He already had a wicked case of cauliflower ear on both sides. Every time I went over there, he was in the middle of working out. Shirtless every time, too, in his humid and sweaty dining room he called a gym. This time was no different. I swear he did that intentionally just to impress me.

My dad taught me how to punch a heavy bag when I was a little kid. That's one of my earliest memories of him. I had no desire to make small talk with this Roy motherfucker, though, so I didn't bring it up.

He gave me the same spiel that he always did: "Yeah, I don't do drugs anymore. I don't smoke weed and only drink in moderation. I just need something to calm me down now and again, or I might punch a hole in a wall. Fighters get like that. You have to get like that if you wanna make it far. I don't look at Xanax as a drug. It's more of a medication."

"I hear ya," I said.

I couldn't stop looking at that nasty-ass cauliflower ear. It was menacing.

I gave him the baggie, and he gave me the money.

"Ey, if you ever wanna work out, lemme know in advance."

"Sure will," I said.

He kept going on like, "Yeah, especially for a dude like you. No offense. Gotta look tough and *be* tough selling shit all day. So, you watch a lot of MMA?"

I thought he said anime. I was under the impression that he assumed I was a nerd just because I was skinny. I was annoyed but too tired to show it. I said, "Nah. I used to watch Pokémon, though."

He was perplexed. "Huh? What?"

How the fuck was this motherfucker gonna ask me if I watched anime but not know what Pokémon was? I was all like, "Pokémon. You've never heard of that?"

He was even more perplexed. This fuckin' knuckle dragger.

He said, "No, I know Pokémon, but what does that have to do with anything?"

"Aren't they both Japanese?"

"Oh," he said. "I mean, well, jujutsu is. But that's just a part of it."

I didn't know what the fuck he was on about, so I was just like, "All right, I gotta get goin' man."

"All right, man," he said, all awkward-like. As if I were the awkward one.

Fuckin' freak, I thought.

I realized he said MMA fifteen minutes later in the car.

◆◆◆

Frank got particularly wild with all these new life changes. He had the money, he had a way with people, and apparently, according to Nora at least, he had good "pipe game." A banger was scheduled at his place.

Before the party started, we all gathered at UB for the

firework show. That was the move in Buffalo. First, you went to UB, then you went to your own clique's party. It was a tradition everyone did.

So, there had to be a couple thousand people there. All drunk, dressed head to toe in American attire. Girls had red, white, and blue makeup and glitter, with short shorts and flip-flops. Dudes had American flag tank tops or were shirtless with equivalent body paint. The more country dudes, the ones from North Tonawanda or some shit, had cowboy boots and bottles of dip spit in their tight ass denim.

Me, Frank, Nora, Walter, and the others found a nice patch of grass and sat down with our beers. Before we knew it, the very first firework popped up into the atmosphere and exploded. Everyone cheered and watched the show.

As all firework shows go, they'd have pockets of mass explosions mixed with moments of nothingness for dramatic effect and whatnot. I must've killed, like, four beers before it was even halfway through, and I really had to pee. I stood up to see if porta potties were lying about. When I stood, I suddenly had to pee ten times more than I did when I was sitting down. I'd experienced that effect before. I think when your guts are scrunched up in a sitting position, you don't feel it as much.

"What is it?" asked Frank.

"Is there a porta potty anywhere?"

None of them knew.

"Shit," I said.

"Just hold it," said Frank.

"I can't."

I left them and entered the massive crowd. The explosions would light the world around me, and for just a second, I saw the visages of hundreds of faces. It was freaking me out. Blackness. Thousands of faces. Blackness. I walked until I kicked something. A girl's voice said, "Ow!"

I kept on, but I couldn't find a fuckin' porta potty.

There were woods along the outskirts of the field, and I felt no choice but to resort to them. I'm sure it looked creepy: this tall, skinny kid venturing into the trees. But when you have to pee that bad, pride no longer becomes a worry.

I crunched through the many twigs, then heard voices. I stopped. I heard voices and pee streams and realized I wasn't alone in this struggle. The forest *was* the porta potty. Many drunk people were peeing here, saying shit about their lives or inside jokes or just how "fucked up" they were. I unzipped and let out my stream. What a feeling. It was comparable to an orgasm. The pee stream rose, and hundreds of hidden mosquitoes buzzed around my head and planted themselves on my skin. It was hard to smack at them when I couldn't see shit. I kept feeling little pinches all over. This was a long one, too. The pee, that is. I had a lot to release.

Now, from behind me, came a voice I knew. A voice I knew but couldn't quite identify. I looked behind me as I peed. An explosion flashed, and the face of A-Rod and Leslie appeared. They were making their way to the woods, talking and laughing. A-Rod looked fresh as can be and Leslie, well, she was dolled up from what I could tell. Almost didn't recognize her at first but staring down a finger gun is hard to forget.

I spun my head back around, flipped my hood up. The longest piss in history wasn't even close to being complete.

A-Rod asked, "You're just gonna piss out here with the guys?"

And Leslie said, "I don't give a fuck."

Yes, it was them. I was sure of it. They sounded drunk, too. They were probably dealing out here all night. I stayed still, listening to how far away they were like some fucking bat, letting my dribbling wiener hang. I heard their footsteps approach, pass me, then move away in front of me. All the while I did not move. I couldn't move. They had me in the woods with nothing but my dick in my hands.

An explosion cracked and lit the woods once again. In that split second, I saw Leslie's bare ass as she squatted there and peed like ten yards in front of me. Blackness again. The sight of it pierced me somehow. Pierced some deep nerve.

I turned and walked fast. I tripped, then ran. I didn't hear their voices again.

♦♦♦

They called me crazy. Said I was just seeing things.

I knew what I saw. I saw Leslie's bare ass. The image of it would not leave me. The bare ass of my enemy, there in the black woods. She had no idea I saw it.

I was all like, "Bro, I swear to God, I saw her bare ass. Her entire bare ass. The entire thing." I made a circle with my finger. "Everywhere I go, they show up. Tim Horton's. The woods. It's a sign. This was a sign. Me seeing her bare ass was a sign."

Frank laughed at me. "What?" he asked. "When did you see them at Tim Horton's?"

"Long time ago. It's all gonna come back to bite us. He hasn't forgotten."

He made a face. "Why are you scared of that bitch? We fucked him up."

"You haven't seen what I've seen."

"You're a bitch, too."

Even Walter, that freak-ass, seemed to agree with him. Nora, as well. I was left there, babbling in a lawn chair outside the house, with God knows how much alcohol coursing through my body. Every word hurt my brain.

I tried to relax and smoked a cigar. It kind of worked, but the image of Leslie's evil ass still popped into my head here and there.

Frank had driven down to Pennsylvania and bought, like, a grand's worth of fireworks. The laws about fireworks were weird in New York. Same with Pennsylvania, so I don't know how he did it. Maybe someone on the inside. I think technically you could own them, but you just couldn't sell them. But then it was illegal to set them off without a permit, but the hogs didn't really give a shit on the Fourth of July. They were probably making money off DUI checkpoints. I don't know.

Anyway, this party. The whole upper class of druggie suburbia was there. Minus the Asians. They never came to our parties after the mugging. Probably for the best.

Frank had it set up real nice with stacks and stacks of thirty-racks, various cheap meats sizzling on the grill, American shit all around. Nora made red, white, and blue weed cupcakes. I stayed away from those. No more weed for me. Lately, it gave me panic attacks. It used to do the opposite. I don't know. People change. Their brains change.

This drunk kid from high school was all like, "Yo, Bobby, is that a Cuban cigar?"

"Honduran," I said.

"What?"

"It's Honduran."

"What's that?"

"Forget it."

"Let me try it."

I gave him the wet, smoking stick and said, "Don't inhale."

He held the whole thing with his thumb and index finger like it was a joint, sucked hard, and certainly inhaled. He coughed all the thick smoke out.

"I told you," I said.

"Bro, how can you *not* inhale what you're smoking?"

I just shrugged my shoulders.

Firecrackers and bottle rockets were popping and screaming from near and far. Frank took that as permission to bring out the big boys. He stuck one of those tubes in the ground and dropped a lit mortar in it. He didn't tell anyone to get back or anything like that. I think that was intentional.

When the wick was up, the mortar went *Foom!* and shot two-hundred feet into the sky and exploded all miraculously. The surprised drunk patrons of this party hollered and clapped.

Some other punk went to the plentiful harvest of explosives and took a whole drum of firecrackers and lit it with the end of his cigarette. They rattled like machine-gun fire for, like, fifteen seconds straight, shooting gunpowder smoke and sparks all around.

That shit was too obnoxious, so I went inside. Some people were sitting around the table with cards and beers and mixed drinks playing some drinking game. I never really liked drinking games. Most of them were more annoying than fun, particularly that flipper-cupper, or whatever. I fuckin' hated that. Fuck that. I preferred to play a relaxing game, like poker or something, while killing beers at my own pace. You feel me?

But I joined the circle of basic motherfuckers regardless—I wasn't gonna just sit in the background like some freak. This was still some of my house, too, and these normies were gonna know it. I lugged that big-ass cigar around, blowing into the kitchen ceiling fan.

One of the little thumb-suckers that I didn't know was all like, "Yo, you're Bobby, right?"

"Yeah," I said.

"You're Frank's boy?"

"Yeah."

He smiled all fucked up-like. "Where them Xans at?" he asked.

The rest of the tiny tots looked at me with their eyes all aglow, finding it hard to party without some Xanax tonight. If I'm being honest, I liked playing the role of an affluent drug dealer. I liked it a lot. So, I said, "Christmas in July. Who wants a bar?"

Four of them did, then another two tagged along, not wanting to appear soft in front of others.

I dug into my pocket gave them all a single unwrapped bar. One of the dudes held up his pill and went, "Cheers!"

We all held the Xannies up in the air, then swallowed.

Now you're really not supposed to mix alcohol with Xanax. It can, like, stop your heart or something like that. But we did it anyway. At this point, these other kids could die, and their ghosts would be in such awe about Santa Washburn, they'd forget they'd died.

Like I said, I never really cared for Xanax alone, but if the night called for mixing it with booze, I was game. You had to mix things up now and again—things got too boring otherwise. If you drank every day, what would your special treat be? Couldn't be alcohol. Even drunks need a special treat.

I was handing out pills much more than I should have, and I was consuming much more than I should have. I lost track after, like, six. Certainly, when you go this hard, one's memory becomes a bit nonuniform. But I remember the mortar exploding in the house.

I stayed inside for most of the party. We were all leaning on the counter and whatnot, drunk as shit, barred out as shit. I'm sure we were slurring hard, talking about absolute nonsense. Making out and blacking out. Outside, they were just as inebriated and still cranking out the fireworks. There was your classic roman candle war, which is often relatively harmless, though still not particularly safe. But with enough drugs and a lack of brain cells, folks started resorting to heavier fireworks to spar with. Now the thing about these mortars is that they can ricochet. I'm told one of these idiots pulled the mortar tube from the ground and used it as his grenade launcher. Luckily, when it *foomed,* nobody got clocked by it. But it hit the fence and deflected and broke through Frank's kitchen window, landing right in front of me. Someone screamed. Someone asked, "Ay, yo, what is that?" Everything went into slow motion. It happened too quickly for me to jump out of the way. I just sort of stepped out of the way. Not nearly far enough away. Certainly not.

The explosion wasn't loud. Well, I'm sure it was, but it fucked up my ears quicker than I could hear. If that makes sense. It was like an elongated muffled bang followed by intense ringing. The shockwave knocked me and the rest of us to the ground. The whole house was black smoke. Everything was black smoke. I fumbled through it all and got out the door and lay in the grass, still deaf. That's when it all started to burn. My eyes were so dry and smoke-stung, it was nearly five minutes before I could finally open them.

My shirt had almost entirely burned off. I had black and scorched blotches of skin.

But I was somewhat okay. When it became clear to me what happened, I stood slowly. The burns hurt really bad, but my limbs and vitals and eyes all seemed to be all right.

The fire department came soon after. They pulled out drunk kids completely covered in black soot with dazed faces. Ambulances came. Neighbors came. The hogs came. Suddenly it was a whole fuckin' spectacle.

The hogs made me nervous, and I couldn't bring myself to think straight, so I just started walking. Every step hurt. I had no idea how long it was going to take, but all I could think about was going home. My apartment, not home-home. Ma couldn't see me like this.

♦♦♦

It was a miracle I made it back. I was in so much fuckin' pain, I was damn near crawling. Some people I passed on the street were scared of me. I must've looked like a fuckin' zombie—burned skin, filthy face, ripped clothes, strange manner of walking, groans.

I slammed the front door and tried to inspect myself in the mirror. The fabric was burned into my skin. Taking off the shirt wasn't too bad, but the jeans were really soldered in there. I was swearing and crying as I forced myself to rip the black, crispy skin off me. You can smell it—burned skin and hair. It made the whole room smell. When they were free, I lay back, naked and spreadeagle. There was some relief, but it all still burned.

Everything in my pockets was miraculously undamaged. I crawled to the kitchenette for the cold tile floor and sat there and smoked one of my cigarettes. Texts were asking if I was alive, where the fuck I was. I told them I was alive and at home, but sort of wished I wasn't.

A cold shower and a cold shower beer helped. The water was black. The bath towels were spotted in blood from when I dried myself.

I hobbled to my shitty bed, pulled a blanket over my naked body, and passed the fuck out for real.

◆◆◆

I jumped awake with fear. This was how it was every morning now. Before bed each night, I laid two Xanax beside my lamp, because I knew what was to come the next morning—terrible, terrible fear. Also known as alcohol withdrawal. My habit had finally caught up to me. I was now the drunk who shakes in the morning, and I wasn't even old enough to grow a full beard. You know that feeling you get when a deer jumps in front of your car? That quick, sinking fear that clenches your heart and guts? That feeling that only lasts a moment? Alcohol withdrawal is just like that, but instead of a moment, it lasts for days. And that's just the worst symptom. You shake. You itch. Electric pulses vibrate every nerve until they hurt. At first, there's hardly anything to be afraid of, yet you're terrified. In time, there are Shadowmen there, and there. Your brain is so chaotic you can barely read a text message. You cannot eat without puking. You cannot sleep. For days. All of this for days.

I chewed the first Xanax and waited ten minutes in my sweat. I chewed the other. Xanax doesn't just help with alcohol withdrawal: it cures it. Problem is, if you keep at it, you'll build a tolerance to the stuff, and then it won't work as well. Then you'll have to detox off both the booze and Xanax simultaneously. I knew all this in the back of my mind, but every time I felt healthy again, I drank. It wasn't like giving in to temptation the way you might think. It felt more robotic. My brain commanded my legs to go to the store. It commanded my hands to grab the beer. It said, *Drink child*. And I did. Somehow it wasn't scary whenever I held that bottle, ready for the first drink of the day, even though I knew the horrific fear was certainly coming because of it.

When the Xanax took its effect, I remembered I was scorched in burns. They didn't feel so bad, though, in comparison to the withdrawal. I drank water and fell back asleep. When I woke again, it was dark. I had no idea how much time had passed. But there was beer in the fridge, and cigarettes on the counter, so I walked all painful-like and drank and smoked.

♦♦♦

Days later, we all gathered around Frank's laptop. My burns were hot and crispy, but I kept a steady supply of aloe to deaden the pain. Walter navigated to the dark web. I was surprised that the interface of the Silk Road looked like any other website. Its emblem was a medieval merchant atop a camel, and beneath that lay rows and rows of drugs for sale. They were advertised all obnoxious-like:

FIRE LEMON KUSH CHRONIC 15 A GRAM.

FLASH SALE! PURE ROXY ROXY ROXY

DMT TABS! TRIP YOUR BALLS OFF

There was other shit, too. Some freak was selling his homemade pretzels on there. Like, not even THC-infused pretzels.

Just normal pretzels.

There was a new kind of Xanax that had found its way into Buffalo. They were called Green Hulks, and they were all rage. Walter looked up Green Hulks in the search bar, and, sure enough, there they were. Chunky green bars, a bit blockier than their white counterparts, with the ID S | 90 | 3 impressed on them. This was perplexing to me at first. Remember, none of this shit is the real deal—they just design pill presses to mimic the real thing. So why would you make fake generic shit? Why not just fake real shit? That's like stealing the display model that's been running every damn day instead of the new one right below it. I'd come to learn it was just a thing of branding. Green Hulks, whether true or false, got labeled as "stronger than your ordinary Xanax", so they sold better. Plain and simple for all the mutants who jumped on and off this drug-laced road.

Anyway, considering the influx of Green Hulks in Buffalo, Frank decided we should invest in some. The real question, though, was if this first wave of Green Hulks didn't come from us, then who did it come from?

Frank was all flustered-like, and asked, "Is it XanRunner96 who's selling them?"

"No," said Walter. "GodOfXanzzz, actually."

"So, who the fuck's been buying them in Buffalo?"

♦♦♦

A week later, we were sitting on Frank's stoop waiting for Craig the mailman with our Green Hulks. The sun roasted my healing burns to the point where it looked like I left stones on my body and laid out for 4 hours. I just lied and said it was some new age thing like Reiki or some shit. The customers didn't ask follow-up questions.

Craig came huffin' and puffin' down the sidewalk. It was hot out. He approached us with the same ol' mantra: "Hey guys."

Frank didn't toy with him. He just said, "Yo."

Craig noticed this new seriousness and didn't know how to respond, so he just didn't. He handed us the package and walked away. I could tell he didn't know if he should say bye or not. Poor guy. Poor, sweaty guy.

Then, tires whined from down the street. In moments, the car was at our driveway and halted instantly, making the heads of A-Rod and Leslie jolt forward and back. Their car was used and cheap and had bald tires that needed air, and it had rust decay on every edge. Perfect for doing crimes in and torching in the woods after. Leslie cranked the window down, poked her head out the window, and said, "Give it to us, and we'll call it even."

Frank stood calmly and held the package of Green Hulks in his hands. He waited a moment, then gently asked, "What now?"

She spat black juice onto the pavement and wiped her lips with her fingers. "Give us your shit, and we don't kill you."

Frank laughed. "This bitch is delusional. Get the fuck out of here before I kill *you*."

A-Rod hollered from the other side, "Who the fuck are you talkin' to?"

Frank said, "You, you and your weird-ass bitch."

A-Rod got out and powerwalked toward Frank with savagery in his eyes. He was unarmed with weaponry but equipped with wounded pride.

Frank tossed the package onto the porch and raised his fists to accept the opponent. A-Rod leveled his fist, and Frank blocked it with his forearm but hollered in pain and backed up, cradling his arm. Frank backed away, confused by the force of one punch. A-Rod pursued. He punched Frank again and again until he caught him in the mouth. A collection of spit, blood, and teeth clacked and splattered onto the driveway. Frank was now downed and screaming my name.

I went to move, but Leslie was upon me, and their secret weapon became revealed. I was wrong. They *were* armed. Both of Leslie's fists were laced in brass knuckles. She swung for my head but caught me in the chest. It felt like I was clubbed by a mace. Then she swung again, and I backed away from it. All the pains of the burns left me, and now the blunt force trauma caused fury to take over. I leaped at her, knocking us over, and I pummeled her hard. She smacked against the concrete, trying to get away. I grabbed hold of her face and squeezed for some reason. The chew in her lip came out, fell between my fingers. All my life, I never laid a hand on a girl, until this moment. But my inebriated, son-of-a-killer instincts kicked in. I kept squeezing her face, hard, without speaking.

A-Rod either kicked me or punched me in the side of the head while I was on top of her, and I blacked out. On the grass, I was taking punches and kicks from both of them. Every time they punched me, my flesh and bones made a squishy sound. I begged them to stop. I said, "All right, all right, just take the shit!"

We were then consumed by a cloud of thick, white haze. It sounded like a hose but felt like sand. It was in my eyes and lungs, but I took the moment to roll to freedom. When I wiped my eyes, I saw A-Rod and Leslie painted white and Walter holding a now-empty fire extinguisher as a defense weapon. He guarded the porch where the pills lay.

The cloud of white still floated. A-Rod coughed a bit and wiped his face. He breathed deeply and went to charge Walter. He lifted his fire extinguisher, ready to heave.

Leslie stopped A-Rod.

"Wait," she said, then pulled out a spring-assisted pocketknife, flicked it open, and came to me.

She took me by the hair and pulled my head up. I groaned as I felt the cold knife on my neck. I could feel it slicing me a little with every deep, terrified breath I took.

She said, "Give us the shit or I kill your little butt buddy here."

Walter did not move immediately. He looked at me. He looked at A-Rod. He looked at me again, then slowly stepped aside. The pills were ripe for the taking.

As A-Rod grabbed the stash from the porch, Leslie continued to hold me with the knife at my throat. She whispered into my ear like a mother whispering to her baby. "Take any of my licks again, and I'll kill you. For a killer's son, you're pathetic, Bobby Washburn." Then, she kissed me on the lips. It tasted like copper and salt. She pulled the knife away and, with A-Rod, escaped with thousands of dollars in profit. Craig the mailman, sweating like a motherfucker in the neighbor's yard, turned and left, all doe-eyed.

Frank was crawling on his hands and knees, groaning, and spitting blood. He and Walter were looking around in the grass for his missing teeth. Like they could be put back in. Meanwhile, I'm sitting there, beat to hell, with little slices on my neck. Despite it all, I realized I just had my first kiss.

III.

I get the call.

"Hello, this is a collect call from Attica Correctional Facility. From inmate, Robert Washburn Sr. Say Yes or press 1 to accept this call."

I did. Garbled sounds hit my eardrum first.

He said, "Hello?"

I said, "Hi."

"What's wrong?"

"What?"

"What's wrong?"

"I didn't say anything was wrong."

"I know, but I can tell."

"You called me," I said.

"What's wrong, Bobby?"

"......"

"What's wrong, Bobby?"

"How do you know when you're in over your head?"

"When you have to ask."

"I think I'm in over my head, Dad"

"What happened?"

"They jumped us with brass knuckles. My face is all fucked up. And I got burns."

"Burns?"

"Well, that's from something else."

"Who jumped you?"

I was talking all fast. "I don't know. The Asians. The fuckin' Asians."

"I don't know what this is referring to, Bobby."

I paused and said, "...you know."

So, he was all stern-like, "Get out of it now."

"It's not that simple. Frank's teeth all got knocked out. He's pissed. He'll have fake teeth for life."

"That's his problem."

"Mine, too."

"How?"

I got a lump in my throat and said, "I don't know. He acts like it's my problem, too."

My dad continued, all like, "I'm telling you, that's how they get you and ruin your life."

I whispered, "It's not a gang."

"Get out of it, now."

"......"

"Bobby."

I said all defeated-like, "I gotta go."

"Bobby."

"......"

"......"

♦♦♦

We both bought shotguns, Frank and me. In New York, you needed a permit to get a handgun, but not a rifle or shotgun. Frank's was black, tactical-looking, and pump-action. It had a pistol grip and a short barrel—better suited for home and drug stash defense.

Mine, on the other hand, was a wooden over-under, better suited for hunting ducks out of the air. At the gun store, I couldn't decide which one I should get. The old man behind the counter said, "The man don't choose the gun. The gun choose the man."

That wooden over-under was the first one I noticed. I knew it wasn't the right fit for what I needed it for, but it just spoke to me. It chose me.

We went out east to where there are woodlands and fewer people. To where the few people who are there tend to love shooting guns themselves. We picked a patch of forest that looked all right and started target practice. Both shotguns were loud and recoiled hard. I loved mine. The whole day I admired it, examined it, caressed it.

We drank our beers and set the empty cans atop a tree stump and blasted them into shreds. That got boring kind of quickly. It's pretty hard to miss with a shotgun if the target isn't moving.

We started tossing full beer cans in the air as skeet. Neither of us were very good at it, but we eventually got one or two.

In time we just sat there in the woods, drinking our beers and smoking cigarettes and cigars. It was fall, and the earthy decay lay beneath us, wet and fragrant. Our spent shells lay there, too. The sky was gray and the trees around us barren, save a few friendless leaves.

"This is nice," I said. "I haven't been out in the woods in years."

"Yeah," said Frank. Each time he took a pull of his beer, I noticed his set of fake teeth. I'm sure they were just a centimeter longer than his real ones, but even that minor change in anatomy was enough to make him look uncanny to me. They weren't right.

I was the first to speak on the topic of our enemies, though I knew we were both thinking it the whole time.

"Now they won't mess with us," I said, and aimed my shotgun at nothing in particular.

Frank was silent for a moment. Then he said, "I'm gonna kill those fuckers." He adjusted a fake tooth with his thumb.

"You know you can't do that," I said.

He did not respond. He did not look this way nor that way. He sat, unblinking, letting his cigarette turn to ash.

"We should make a fire," I said, looking at Frank, waiting for him to respond.

Finally, he acknowledged me. "Go ahead."

I gathered as many dry sticks as I could find. I piled them into a teepee and stuck straw and the cardboard of a cigarette pack inside. I lit it and let the paper burn, then I blew until the straw was alight, and soon the droplets of water inside the sticks were popping and the wood took flame. I gathered larger sticks and was startled by a porcupine that had been there for I don't know how long.

"Frank, look."

He came, and we observed the fat, little critter. They look like a cross between a caterpillar and a beaver. A big rodent with spikes protruding from it every which way. It surely noticed us but was unbothered. It poked its nose into the dirt and sniffed, pursuing grubs and acorns or whatever the hell porcupines eat.

"I can't believe the gunshots didn't scare it away."

A horrible grin exposed. Frank's fake teeth all mannequin-lookin'. He aimed his shotgun at the animal.

"Don't," I said.

He smiled more and closed one eye.

"Frank, *don't*."

I went to take the gun from him, but he stepped away and continued his aim. I pursued him. I took hold of the barrel, and he shoved me back hard. He aimed it again and fired. The creature damn-near exploded and sent an array of bodily shrapnel all over. It splattered onto the trees. It splattered onto our shoes and faces.

Then it was silent, and the remaining shredded carcass lay smoking.

Frank pumped the shotgun and sent the used shell twirling. He was smiling as he saw what he'd done. "Holy shit," he said.

I charged him and plowed my head into his chest, and it took us both to the ground. We grunted and wrestled with the shotgun fumbling around in between us, safety off. I punched at him, but he got ahold of me and flipped me over. Our arms were stiff, trying to outmaneuver each other like subdued wrestlers. But he got the best of me and soon had his bicep wrapped around my neck. Headlock. I squirmed but could not go anywhere. I was letting out this childish, whiny breath of frustration.

Finally, I stopped squirming. "Let me go," I gasped.

"You good?" he asked.

"Yeah."

"You sure?" He squeezed tighter. I tapped on his forearm. I surrendered.

"Yes," I cried.

He let go, and I jumped free. Then we both stood there awkwardly, covered in wet leaves and dirt, breathing hard.

"Why the fuck did you do that?" I asked.

"Who cares?"

"It wasn't doing anything."

He laughed at me. "Bobby, do you know how many gophers there are in the world? Who the fuck cares?"

I was silent. Then said softly, "It wasn't a gopher."

"Huh?"

Even softer, I said, "It was a porcupine."

"Huh?"

"I hate you. I always have."

♦♦♦

I heard her hollerin' before I saw her. Ma, that is.

I pulled up on the house, and there she was, screaming out the window at Gerald. I parked and got out.

Gerald was all like, "Relax! Relax!" as he dodged the twirling spatula flying out the window. Her aim was terrible.

Ma was so pissed. I couldn't even make out what she was saying. A meat tenderizer came soaring out, and he dodged that, too. "Jesus Christ," he hollered, then ran for cover behind his truck.

Ma poked her witchy head out the window, her hair all mangled and what have you. She said, "Yeah, you better hide, motherfucker." She noticed me but didn't acknowledge me. It was clearly an inconvenient time for me to randomly show up after months of no communication. She went back into the house, holler-mumblin' some nonsense.

Gerald poked his head up from behind the truck.

I said, "Damn, Gerald. What did you do?"

He raised his hands and shoulders all confused-like, then went to say something but didn't say anything. He seemed kind of guilty. He hopped in his truck and started it up.

As he was backing up, Ma came out with a can of soup and screamed, "Don't come back! I'm done with you!" then shot-put the can of soup through his fuckin' windshield. It must've clonked him in the head or something because he stepped on the gas and drove the bed of his truck right into the neighbor's tree. He threw it into drive and was gone. His taillight was shattered.

Ma stood there in the driveway. We locked eyes.

"Well, look what the fuckin' cat dragged in," she said.

Apparently, Ma caught Gerald sexting some other woman. He sent this woman a photo of him naked, lying down in bed all seductive-like. That made me laugh and quiver at the same time. It was a unique sensation. I couldn't get the image out of my head for quite some time.

Ma was drinking again, of course, which I was actually happy about because I really wanted a drink myself. The strange thing about Ma and I was that we could forgive each other without saying so. She gave me a White Trash Mimosa and gave herself one, too, and we both knew that things were once again cool between us. I don't know. We both didn't fuck with the mushy apologetic shit.

Then, Ma said, "What are you kids doing these days? That cupping stuff? Your skin looks like shit."

♦♦♦

But I still partied at Frank's new place that night. I was hungover in the morning, but not dope sick. I had enough Xanax in me. I woke with half my body underneath the couch, the other half covered in a fallen window curtain. I must've burrowed beneath the couch for warmth and wrapped myself in anything available. I remembered little. A fragment here and there. Whatever. Memory was useless in pain such as this. It felt like I was void of moisture from my tongue down to my asshole. I felt like I was going to vomit ash.

I slithered from my trashy glen and made my way to the sink in a befuddled stumble. In the sink was a pool of some liquid that perplexed me. Nonetheless, I stuck my head under the faucet and drank. My throat was so fuckin' dry that it hurt to swallow the first few times. It was certainly the best water I had ever drank, though. Yes. Absolutely. That liquid in the sink was splashing into my ear, but I couldn't have cared less. Water. Yes. Amazing water.

When my belly was fat, I lifted my head and wiped my lips with my forearm. Of course, though, as any hangover goes, I still felt like shit. I just wasn't thirsty anymore. Now I wanted to urinate and inhale nicotine.

I went to open the bathroom door, but it got caught by something. I poked my head in to see that that something was the body of a person I'd never seen in my life. Big, hairy motherfucker. Hair that was now mangled all over the floor. He was dressed in black like he was a diehard Metallica fan or some shit. Some girl was in there, too, awake, puking into the toilet bowl.

"You okay?" I asked.

She turned around and showed me her face of immense torment. "Yeah," she said, with vomit-infused drool hanging from her mouth.

"Is that guy okay?" I nodded toward the man who I wasn't sure was alive or dead.

"Yeah, Ray's just sleeping."

"Well, all right," I said.

She stuck her head back in the toilet, and I went out the backdoor to pee outside. It was very chilly, which felt somewhat relieving on my boiling head. I picked a patch of grass that lay riddled with cobbled concrete, unzipped my jeans, and let out a hot, dehydrated stream of urine. Neon fuckin' yellow. That water hadn't hit my bladder yet.

I was done quickly. I jiggled, then zipped back up. That entire time there was a man on the other side of the steps who I hadn't noticed until I turned back around. Another Metallica fan lookin' motherfucker. Where were all these Metallica fans coming from? We made eye contact, and he smiled, exhaling his cig smoke, then said, "What's up Fig Newton?"

I said, "What's up," all uncomfortable-like.

It sounded like he called me Fig Newton, and if he did, I had no fuckin' clue what that meant. I didn't even know who this guy was. But I was cautious to ask. Say he didn't actually call me Fig Newton, and I were to say, *Did you just call me Fig Newton?* I would sound like I was out of my Goddamn mind.

But then I thought, *Who the fuck cares?* A hangover has a way of making you paranoid, yet also careless of ego. I don't know.

"Did you just call me Fig Newton?" I asked.

He grinned. "Blacked out, eh?"

"Apparently."

"Do you even remember me?" he asked.

"Yeah," I said, though I didn't. "I just don't remember the Fig Newton bit."

"Well, you were eating Fig Newtons. That was it."

"Oh."

"Yeah."

"Well, that was an underwhelming reveal."

"What?" he said.

He probably didn't know what underwhelming meant, though that's one of the most self-explanatory words I can think of. Party folk are often brick dumb.

I pulled out a cigarette from my pack. Pall Mall. Red.

We stood in silence just smoking, observing this ratty backyard that wasn't given any care since the 70s. A return to the natural plants and weeds and all that yuppie stuff.

Metallica Boy 2 threw his cig butt to the ground and stomped it. He dug into his pocket and pulled out a sandwich bag of powdery crystals. The bag didn't even have a zip. It was one of those fold-over ones. He took a little scoop from the bag with his long nails and sucked it up his nose.

I watched him all curious.

He put the bag back in his pocket and brought his arms back to his sides as if nothing about what he just did was askew.

"Did you just do meth?" I asked.

"Yeah."

"Oh."

"What?"

"I don't know...just...nothing. I wasn't expecting that."

"The media kind of exaggerates it. It's basically just stronger Adderall or Vyvanse that hits you like a damn truck."

I contemplated. That didn't sound too bad. "Really?" I asked.

"Yeah. Immediately kills a hangover, too. Immediately."

"Huh."

♦♦♦

So just like that, I was doing fuckin' meth. I had done a lot of drugs before this one, but truth be told, I have never felt a euphoria comparable to the first time I sucked that shit up my nose. It was like whatever hormone makes you happy was radiating through my veins for damn near a whole hour. My heart was racing, but it felt good. Really good. And certainly, that wasn't the end of it. No, no. This shit lasts a while. Maybe not the intense euphoria, but all the other tweaky effects keep going strong.

I had this urge to write like I'd never had before. I took Frank's crusty-ass laptop and just started typing away at a story. It was certainly really, *really* bad writing. But at the moment, I felt like fuckin' Hemmingway.

The whole house remained hungover while Metallica Boy 2 and I did meth all morning long. I was in utter bliss typing away at the keyboard, smoking cigarettes until I didn't have any left. Metallica Boy 2 was playing some game on his phone.

"Yo," I said to him after I wrote, like, damn-near seven pages. "I like this stuff."

"Yeah, it's pretty nice," he said.

"You got a connect?"

"Yeah."

♦♦♦

We bought more, and by the time we got back, everyone was up, and they all tried meth, too. I was fixated on that laptop. Tapping away and shit. I was sucking down beer, and that combined with the meth made me feel like a powerhouse of a writer. I felt amazing. This was what I was born to do. I was writing the next Great American Novel while still in my twenties. The story was about a gunslinger who traveled from Buffalo to the Southwest. Some poor attempt at being Cormac McCarthy. I cringe thinking back on it.

Cranked out, Frank was all like, "Bobby, what are you doing?"

"Writing," I said, not taking my eyes from the screen.

He observed me for some moments, all hungry-like, then said, "Let me try."

The thought of giving up the laptop made me feel bad. All of a sudden, I felt bad. What could I say, though? It was his laptop, after all.

I was all like, "Just let me finish this next chapter."

"All right," he said, eyes still on me.

Now I couldn't focus. I was out of the cowboy dream world and this newly-cranked-out fucker Frank was watching the laptop like it was some enchanted ornament. Suddenly, the story wasn't right. The characters weren't working. The plot was cliche. So cliche! I highlighted the entire thing and hit Delete, then Undo, then Delete again, then closed the laptop and said to Frank, "It's all yours."

He took it eagerly and opened it up. Almost immediately he was typing. I'm certain it was garbage worse than mine.

Frank shut the laptop, too. "I'm not liking this," he said. "Do you want to fight again? Or play football?"

He stood up.

"I need to move," he said. "I need to *do* something."

He went to the pile and snorted a bump himself, all heavy-like. He said, "Ahhh," then flexed his muscles and clenched his fake teeth. Then some crazed screamed.

I sensed dangerous forthcomings.

♦♦♦

It was night quicker than it usually is. Amphetamines have a way of doing that. Frank did invite a bunch of people over to play football but soon lost interest before they even arrived. So instead, everyone just partied some more.

The meth had gotten to poor little Walter. I knew it would. Thankfully, we had such a hefty load of Xanax, he was able to calm down rather quickly. The whole time he was on the crank, he was scratching himself and jolting his eyes to the left and right as if something had startled him.

At some point during the party, Metallica Boy 1 started telling me and Frank about the sexual side of meth. He said it was pretty ordinary for meth heads to watch porn for literally five days straight. Maybe even longer.

Like a Goddamn bell ringing, Frank and Nora went upstairs. I knew what they were doing. We all knew. Some of the boys cheered Frank on. It bothered me. It shouldn't have bothered me, but it bothered me. I was a virgin. I didn't want to envision it, but I couldn't help envisioning it. I was standing there at the beer pong table, drunk fucks hollerin' all around me, but my eyes were fixed on nothing save the images in my head. Nora naked. White breasts. I got an erection. I didn't want an erection, but I got an erection. I wanted to cum, and I wanted to hurt someone, and I wanted to dig a bunch of holes in the backyard, for hours—days. I didn't know what I wanted. It was a terrible feeling.

I didn't want meth anymore. No.

I swallowed three Xanax to counteract it. I wanted to be free of this shit. I wanted it gone. I needed sleep. Yes. Certainly.

Then I got to thinking. I could just jerk off and be free of the weird sexual jealousy. By the time I was finished, then the Xanax would've kicked in, and I could sleep this terrible state away.

Yes. It was a great plan.

I went to the bathroom, locked the door behind me. I went to the toilet and started to unzip but stopped. I checked to make sure the door was locked. It was locked. My pants soon fell to my ankles. I started jerking it off, envisioning Nora naked. Her white breasts. Ass just the same. I'd seen what sex looked like from the Internet. I was hard again and started stroking rapidly, but then I stopped. Leaving my pants at my ankles, I waddled over to the door, this rock-hard erection careening in front of me. The handle was locked. Started stroking again.

Ninety seconds into masturbation and you can usually tell if it's gonna be a quicky or a long process. This was gonna be a long process. I heard stomping outside the door. The crank likely slowed down this sort of thing and got me paranoid. My wrist was getting tired, but I powered through. It wasn't doing much good, though, because I'd lost the naked imagery. I had to achieve orgasm. I had to. You can't just get it started then give up. Then it would eat at me all night. I wouldn't be able to sleep. I don't know.

Maybe I could with the Xanax. The Xanax! The Xanax was going to kick in any minute. I had to finish. I was moaning, but not like a sexual moan, like a moan you make when you can't do any more pushups. I had to stop. My forearm couldn't move anymore. So, I switched hands. My left felt unnatural, but I suppose it worked fine in a pinch. White breasts. Flopping white breasts with a flawless ass and moaning and blowjobs and stuff and love...

Someone tried the door, then knocked.

All I could think to say was, "I'm...I'm...I'm taking a SHIT!"

Walter's voice from behind the door said, "Oh. Sorry."

I continued with my right hand. It had had a long enough break. But I felt like the presence of Walter hadn't left. I felt like he was just standing at the door, waiting, listening.

"Walter," I said.

There was no answer.

"Walter," I said louder.

No answer.

I was alone. It took about five more minutes, but I finally did it. It shot out onto the top of the toilet, then dripped around the rim. My heart was fuckin' pounding. My face was hot and flushed.

My mouth was dry. My forearms were already fuckin' sore. My dick felt like I just stuck it in the microwave and hit defrost. I don't know.

I pathetically wiped the cum away with toilet paper, flushed, got a drink from the sink, and exited as if nothing were awry.

As soon as I sat on the couch, I envisioned Nora and Frank again. Sure could hear them, too.

♦♦♦

The Xanax did its job, and I was out cold early into the night. At some point, I must've gotten up off the couch and gone to one of the upstairs bedrooms, but I did not recall doing so. When I woke, it was still dark, and everyone was asleep.

I went downstairs to find a few silhouettes of sedated bodies sprawled out on the floor like dead phantoms. Like statues upon a medieval tomb or some shit.

I went to the fridge, and there were no beers left. They didn't start selling beer until, like, 7 am. It was 4 am. Too long of a wait. Far too long.

I looked deeper within the fridge of crusty food stains and month-old Tupperware filled with gray and brown chunks that were once some meals. There was a tallboy of Peach Twisted Tea. Yes. I enjoyed the occasional Twisted Tea, although they gave me heartburn. But heartburn was the least of my worries in times such as these. When you're addicted to a substance that gives you horrifying withdrawals daily, you become significantly resilient to things that normal people bitch about. Like heartburn.

I took the cold tall can and cracked her open, took a nice hit. There was nearly no light save the bright shine from the refrigerator and the invasive streets lights that came in through the windows. I could just see a little sliver of Frank's carton of Seneca Reds behind all the clutter on the top of the fridge.

What a lucky morning. I stole a pack then smacked it against my palm a few times, jamming the tobacco nice and tight. I opened it up, picked a cigarette at random, and put it back in upside down. My lucky cigarette. It was a little ritual some smokers did. I had forgotten about it for a while, but this stroke of fortune brought it back to me.

I leaned against the counter, lit my smoke, sipped my Twisted Tea, watched the darkness, and enjoyed this moment of peace I hadn't had in so long.

Ah.

Then there was movement. All the peace left me, and I suddenly became hyperaware. It was the sound of someone moving. Someone had gotten up or had been there the whole time. They were coming around the corner. They were coming. Should I say something? I was just standing there in the dark. Would I startle them?

I remained quiet, then the glow of crazed eyes appeared in the blackness. Crazed, meth eyes, and nothing more. They looked at mine.

"Yo," I said.

"What are you doing?" asked Frank. His voice was serious, not curious.

"Just having a smoke."

He stared at me for some moments, then said, "I thought someone broke into the house."

He was holding his shotgun.

He flicked the light on, and the grimy, messy kitchen was now aglow with yellow fluorescence. Frank stood in the door frame, his hair and skin shiny with grease, the gun held tightly in his hands. Thankfully, it was pointed to the floor.

"Frank, you all right?" I asked.

"You startled me."

"Well, sorry."

"Are those my cigarettes?"

"Yeah. I'll pay you back."

"Yeah," he said, then ventured back into the darkness. "We have to be careful, Bobby. Who knows what'll happen next?"

♦♦♦

A bender is much like a dream. They begin without you realizing it. At some point, you're just there, and though most of it is ludicrous, it all feels quite ordinary. Then suddenly, you're awake, and all but the most horrific images stay forever forgotten in the slew of madness. The days went by like a muddy creek. I guzzled a few cases of beer. I swallowed countless Xanax from our supply. I smoked nearly two cartons of cigarettes. I spent well over a thousand dollars. I barely ate. Eventually, I left Frank's house and went to the grimiest bars in all of Buffalo—the ones your mother warned you about. Visages of unshaven men and wrinkly women cackling with wet lips in the ill-lit rooms. I was among them. I told them I was an alcoholic. Many said they were, too. Many looked uncomfortable. At these bars, the bartenders were just as drunk as the patrons. I was vomiting in the bathroom. I switched to whiskey sours. There was a scrum that I was too drunk to even notice at first. Brawny men threw fists and wrestled like half-tranquilized gorillas. The bouncer, big as shit, couldn't even subdue the mosh pit of violence. The hogs came, and I was gone with a man I had just met whose name has become lost in the fog. He was short and stout and had a thin beard poorly disguising acne scars. We ventured through the boondocks until we were in his apartment that was reeking of decaying things. We went through the littered living room to the kitchen where he told me all the booze was stored. That's why I was over there, I believe, initially, for a drink. When the stout man ignited the kitchen light, we found a drunk giant asleep on the floor. His dry and languid eyes cracked open just a bit when the lights came on. Stout man was all like, "Horndorfer! What are you doing in here Horndorfer?" Horndorfer was fucked up and went back to rest. Stout Man smiled at me, explaining that Horndorfer did that sometimes. I wasn't confused then, but I am now. We took liquor to the living room and sat. I listened to Stout Man talk about himself. I suddenly realized it was a mistake. This man was annoying. I told him that I was a writer, and he told me that he was, too. He went to his bedroom and brought back a journal and started reading me his poems. They were so bad, I wanted to cry. He took his time and spoke about each poem as if he were reading to a crowd at a coffee shop. I was the only one in the crowd, and I hated him. Then came the sound of the microwave, and Stout Poet hollered, "Horndorfer! What are you doing?" There was no answer. After the ding, the obese man appeared with a ham and cheese Hot Pocket on a plate. He slit the Hot Pocket open and drank its innards as if it were a Go-Gurt. Big gulps. Stout Poet watched him the whole time, snickering. "Classic," he said. "Classic." Horndorfer was done, then belched a belch so monstrous I felt its wind gust. Soon I was back on the streets, walking with a calm step. Determination reeks of nervousness in dangerous streets such as these. I arrived at my apartment. I was mildly dope sick, so I took a Xanax and fell asleep, then rose again and began drinking. A client came by, and I sold him a fat bag of bars. I had so many pills, so much cash. I felt like a fuckin' king. I stared at myself in the mirror, my blushed face. I felt the stubble on my chin. I liked what I saw, somehow. I went back to Frank's, and he had been awake this whole time. He kept on with the meth and started going nuts. He'd check the windows, stack shit in front of the windows, and then he'd check again. He took the table and flipped it on its side, and I asked why, and he said it was in case of a drive-by. I told him that was unlikely, and he told me I was wrong. He reminded me of the revenge again, and I tried to talk him out of it, and I tried to talk him out of the meth, too. He said he wasn't on any. He was on *plenty*. Later that night, Frank and I went out to drink. To get away from all the meth and chaos. He drank sheepishly. An alcoholic watches how much everyone else drinks. He drank sheepishly. I watched. We went to bars with younger crowds, and I tried to pick up girls but did not succeed. They always seemed repulsed by me. I didn't know how to start a conversation. I found a forsaken pack of cards on a bar table, and I started showing magic tricks to random girls. None were impressed. I kept messing the tricks up. They're harder to do when you're drunk, and I hadn't done them in so long. I'd say, "Is *this* your card?" And they'd say, "No." I gave up and went back to the only thing that seemed to love me well. I took shots of Fireball—not because I'm a bitch, but because they were having some special. I was collapsing backward, and the bouncers tossed me into the street. I woke at Frank's again and vomited but didn't feel better. I drank four screwdrivers and vomited those and then felt better. It was cold, but I still walked to the liquor store in a wifebeater. White trash. I bought rum because I hadn't had rum in quite some time, and a new taste would make me less prone to vomiting. The store was full of wine snobs in cardigans and shit like that. The cashier gave me her smug glower, but I didn't give a shit. I found it funny. On the way back, there was some Vietnam vet with a vicious pit bull on a short chain. The man in his tattered camouflage jacket asked me to give him money to feed his dog so I did. The pit bull was the strongest dog I'd ever seen, fight-marred and grim. I was surprised it didn't maul me when I handed the man a 20. He said, "God Bless." And I said, "I need it." And he said, "It'll come." Soon, Frank's house turned into a nest of immense litter and horrible fragrances. I was among it for days. Who knows how many? There was a stretch where Frank slept, and then he woke again, and he ate, then went back to the crank. Nora was finally concerned, but he just ignored her, and that was the end of it. Maybe two nights later, he took me to his room that was lit by nothing except his laptop screen. He had been watching videos of death. There was one, in particular, he wanted me to see. It was so crazy that he wanted me to see it. The Cartel had flayed all the skin off a man's head and face, leaving behind this muscley, eyeless thing. Its hands were chopped off, and now one of the perpetrators was trying to remove the head from the neck with a dull blade. Another perpetrator held the limp, gory head with his hand. He held it in place for his friend. They were speaking Spanish. Classic rock was playing in the background. Here's the crazy part though: he wasn't dead. The man with no skin on his face was still alive. He let out bizarre gurgles and pleas and tried to reach for his throat with his phantom hands. They were trying and trying to cut off his head, but it wasn't working. All the while, the flayed man swung his flesh head around and tried to rip his stubs from the ropes that held them. Frank watched attentively as if it were a sport. The man was still alive when the video ended. Technically it wasn't a video of death. Frank said, "Isn't that crazy?" And I said, "Yeah." He said, "That's the kind of shit I'm gonna do to that Asian motherfucker. I'm gonna cut his fuckin' face off." He felt his fake teeth with his finger. After that night, I was home for days but continued drinking. I had nightmares I can't remember. I sat at my laptop and constantly talked myself out of looking for that video again. I can't explain it, but some part of me wanted to look. It couldn't have been real. It couldn't have. Yes, it could. It was. Don't watch it again. Don't. Just forget about it. I could never forget about it. I puked on myself and thought I was going to cry but didn't. I ate a handful of Xanax and woke up a day later with pinecones in my bed. I went through my text messages to try to decipher the origin of these pinecones, but I never figured it out. There were at least thirteen of them. Big and sticky. I had to wash my bedsheets thereafter. I went to an Applebee's and ate quesadillas that tasted like they were heated in a microwave. The best quesadillas I'd ever had. I ordered a beer. It was good. I felt all right. The Applebee's started getting kind of crowded. There was a Bills game about to begin. I didn't even know it was Sunday. At first, nobody spoke to me, but once they got enough beers in them, they treated me as if I was one of them. Preps. Braydens and Kaylees. This punk started talking to me about Xanax as if I knew nothing about it. I played along. He was all like, "Yeah, bro, I just took a chip out of one bar, and I was fuuucked." I was all like, "Oh wow." Smug and shit. So, this was what it was like to secretly be a drug dealer. It was a new season, but the Bills still played horribly, as always. People were getting mad. I knew little to nothing about football, but I'd throw out random opinions to hear how these shallow motherfuckers would respond. I'd say, "Drew Bledsoe was the best quarterback the league ever saw." And they'd be like, "What?" And I'd say, "No, I'm dead serious." They'd be all hot and bothered. "Stats mean nothing," I'd say. "It's all about heart." I drove home extremely drunk. Post-Bills game drunk driving is some of the riskiest. The hogs are on the prowl. Very risky, but I was a pro. I went to my desk, uncorked some wine bottle I had. I wrote poetry that was bad but better than that stout motherfucker. Much better. I tried a short story, but it wasn't working, so I went back to poetry. I tried listening to music and smoking cigarettes. I only liked music when I was intoxicated. I woke with my head on the desk, a puddle of drool lying there with me. Who knew how many hours it had been? I felt bad, though. I went to the fridge and poured myself a shot of rum. I threw it back but gagged horribly. I started making the nasty groans of a dog who's about to puke while you're on the brink of sleep after a long day. I forced myself to not and chugged water from the sink. I couldn't get away from the writing, though. I tried again, for days, alone, with my alcohol and puke. I didn't eat. I fell asleep without realizing it. I awoke and did it again. Frank texted me, *Where are you?* It was night. I said, *My crib*. He said, *Coming*. I said, *Why? What's up?* And he didn't respond. I hardly had time to finish my cigarette before he texted me again, saying, *Here*. It was just Frank in his car. I got in and my hands were shaking, but it wasn't the withdrawal this time. "What's up?" He did not speak, just drove. His meth-dried eyes did not lose focus on the night in front of him. Soon we were in the city, and I was all like, "Frank, where the fuck are we going." He calmly replied, "I know where he is." I asked, "Where who is?" And he said, "You know." I'd never had to pee so badly in my life. We came to Jim's Steakout that was brightly lit, and it was crowded with intoxicated patrons. Always was. We parked and waited and watched. "He's in the Jim's?" I asked. "Yes," he said. "How do you know?" He waited a moment, then said, "I saw it on his Instagram." I told myself to just open the door and walk, there wasn't much time. Just open the door and leave, get out of it, like Dad said. I was going to get a job. Pursue writing. Go to college. Get all the degrees I could. I don't fuckin' know. I was done. This was getting way over my head. No breaking even. I was done. Then Frank said, "There he is." He pointed just ahead and there came A-Rod stepping onto the sidewalk with some friends, a bag of hot food in his hand. Frank got out of the car, but I didn't. I froze up. My blood was telling me to get up, go and run. But I didn't. I couldn't move. A-Rod didn't run. He stood his ground. At first, their words came from threatening smiles, but soon they turned to shouts. Get out. Run. Leave. But to my surprise, Frank just came back into the car. I was overreacting. He was cranked out and acting squirrelly. This was just a little tussle of words and nothing more. But then Frank opened the window and was all like, "Do something, pussy." That pissed A-Rod off. He dropped the food and stomped to the car. What was odd about Frank's words was that they did not seem to be a product of anger. They seemed methodical as if this was the next step in the process. His face was calm. His teeth were not clenched. This was his bait. His call. He drew in his prey. As A-Rod approached, Frank stretched into the back seat and pulled out his shotgun that had been lying there in the dark, unnoticed by me until now. "Don't!" I screamed, but the gun exploded and blew half of A-Rod's face off. As he flew back in a twirl, both his hands reached for his face that was not there anymore. His fleshy head twitched a bit, and so did his arms and fingers and legs. Then he died in the street. The shot was loud. I went partially deaf. People were screaming through the ringing, though. Frank handed me the shotgun, and he peeled away. After some time, I heard his voice through my deafened ears. He was all like, "I told you."

♦♦♦

The minute I was dropped off, my pills were flushed down the toilet. My cash was buried out in the woods. I contemplated tossing my shotgun, but that would imply it was the murder weapon if found. I held it, stared at it, stroked its wooden stock, then put it back in the closet. It didn't matter, though. They were going to catch us. No doubt in my mind. This was child's play for a detective. All they'd have to do was ask a few of A-Rod's friends, check surveillance camera for Frank and the car, and we'd be caught. Maybe I could feign innocence and get downgraded to conspiracy at most. Say he was on meth and shit. No drugs on me.

But it was true. Frank threw away our lives. This shit looked worse than my dad's case. If for some reason the death penalty was reinstated, Frank would be eating a couple thousand volts in the electric chair. Honestly, I'd prefer that to life in prison. I wanted to Google search the maximum sentence for conspiracy to commit murder, but I was too paranoid that that would incriminate me further.

The dope sickness hadn't hit me yet, or maybe it wasn't going to at all. I felt strange. I don't know. I think they call that shock. And like all cases of it, it wasn't permanent. I got back into Sheila for what seemed like the last time and drove off. I couldn't stay there in the apartment. I just couldn't, for some reason. Somewhere along the drive to Ma's house, the fear took hold of me.

I tried to take deep breaths, but they supplied no comfort. The full panic attack was upon me. I pulled up on the street and power-walked into my mom's house. I walked in, and Gerald was there in the kitchen.

"Hey, Bobby," he said.

I said nothing and went straight for the fridge. There were only those Mike's Harder Lemonades.

The liquor cabinet was empty. Catherine was squawking.

"Where's the liquor?" I asked Gerald.

"Well, hello to you, too," he said.

"Where's the fucking liquor, Gerald?"

"Your mother dumped it. She's sober again."

"Fuck," I said, and took three of the Mike's Harder's upstairs with me.

"Yeah, you can just have those," hollered Gerald. "That's fine."

I couldn't have cared less. Things didn't seem to change between him and Ma, but shit has gone haywire for me. I would've done significantly worse things to not feel the way I was feeling.

In the hallway upstairs, I walked past Ma, and she asked, "What's wrong?"

"You know what's wrong," I said. Fellow drunks can see withdrawal.

She didn't respond. She understood.

I locked my old bedroom door behind me, cracked a Mike's, chugged, but gagged. This was now much more than a panic attack. My hands were shaking so violently, I could barely bring the can to my lips. I had to hold it with both hands as if it were some holy goblet. I glugged two mouthfuls and gave up. It tasted so synthetic, and my stomach had been void of food for days. The sugary drink loitered in the bottom of my belly and made the dope sick nausea even more intense. It had to get in me, though. It had to. I lifted the can once again and forced down almost all of it. My belly was popping with carbonation, and I blew outward in hopes that it would make me burp faster.

The fear and the trembling had gone nowhere. There was no relief. I gave it a couple of minutes but only felt worse if anything. One can wasn't enough. I cracked open the next, this time letting out horrible groans. My gut and throat were saying no, but my petrified brain was saying, *Please, please, drink, for the love of fucking God, get drunk now*. I wasn't even a quarter of the way through when I puked it all up. All of it. That whole first can was now soaking into the rug.

Why did I flush the Xanax? Why? Couldn't I have just saved one or two?

But it was all gone. All of it down the toilet. And there was no use in trying to drink these Mike's Harder's again. I was going to have to go cold turkey.

It took about five hours for me to start hallucinating. Before that, I lay in my old bed, engulfed with terror, shaking uncontrollably, sweating so profusely that it was soaking through my sheets. There was no getting comfortable. I flopped around and prayed.

That terrible sinking of the heart. My tendons were weak and wobbly. I could hardly breathe. Hours and hours and hours.

I couldn't keep water down, but I was so thirsty my tongue was turning to stone. I was having delusions. This kid, Jimmy Griffin, was at my door. Why would he come? I hadn't spoken to him since 4th grade before he moved to Spain. Now? *Now* he decides to visit me. Why was he ringing the doorbell? Who put a doorbell on my bedroom door? It was so rude for him to come without warning me, without letting me know. I couldn't take the company.

No. What?

No one was at the door, except a demon. Or a ghost. A man. A thing. No, a demon. A robed demon taller than the door. His hermit hair just rubbed against the ceiling. So tall. So incredibly tall and not human but still human. He was going to cut me. He told me. I swear he told me.

I peed my pants, and then jizzed my pants. Then, I vomited. The demon wasn't gone.

They call this level of withdrawal "seeing pink elephants." I saw a demon instead.

◆◆◆

It was maybe a full day before I could stand. The bed was soaked in every bodily waste you can imagine.

I went to the bathroom sink and drank buckets worth of tap water. For maybe a second or two, I felt better, but then the fear had come right back. There was no getting used to this.

I lay on the bathroom floor in my disgusting clothes. My murder outfit and likely the last pair I'd wear before the jumpers. I would go to prison. The detectives would be at my door any minute now, and I'd be taken just like this.

I vomited some of the water into the toilet bowl.

Ma came knocking on the door, all like, "Bobby. Bobby. Are you okay?"

"No," I cried.

She came in and embraced me, then pulled away when she caught my smell. "Jesus Christ," she said.

"I screwed up, Ma," I said, sobbing and shaking beside the toilet.

"I'm taking you to the emergency room."

"No."

"Bobby, I'm taking you to the emergency room. You could have a seizure."

She was right, but I kept on saying no. Something about any sort of government-run facility gave me a sense of handing myself over. Not that hospitals are exactly government-run. In that state of mind, it felt no different than getting arrested. In hindsight, it probably would've been for the best. They probably would've given me Ativan or some shit. Would've made the detox a hell of a lot less nightmarish. But I just couldn't agree to it. No hospitals. No jails. I only had so much freedom left.

"I really screwed up, Ma," I said.

"It's okay, Bobby. I've been here, too. It happens."

"No, that's not what I mean."

"What do you mean?"

"Frank did something real bad."

"What did Frank do?"

I couldn't tell her, but I really wanted to. I wanted to tell her because the fragment of a child that was left in me felt as if telling my mom would make it go away. She'd fix it and then hug me. Everything would be okay. She was my mother. She'd fix it.

But I was no boy anymore. Telling her would just make her an accomplice. She tried to get it out of me, but I didn't let her.

"All you need to know is that I might be in a lot of trouble," I said.

That didn't satisfy her. How could it? I kind of regretted bringing it up in the first place, but at least now she wouldn't be completely surprised when the hogs showed up.

Gerald knocked on the door. He said, "Hey guys, uh, mind if I hop in the shower?"

"Get the hell out of here, Gerald," said Ma.

"Geez. All right. Sorry."

She went back to me and said, "At least clean yourself, Bobby. You're gonna get some sort of infection."

"Okay," I said.

◆◆◆

They call it "windows and waves." During horrific detoxes, you get moments of clarity. Moments where you don't feel like you're dying. Moments where you say, *Phew, okay, it's finally over.*

But then the fear hits again, damn near worse than it did before.

I don't know which is the window and which is the wave, but when I was talking to my mom, I felt better. Then a minute or two into the shower, my heart started pounding, and I was once again crippled by terror.

The bathtub was still fucked up and felt like it was about to fall through the floor any minute. The showers in prison are what I deathly feared. My dad never said anything about it because he's a tall, hard motherfucker. I'd be raped. Bitches get raped. I was a bitch. I'd have to wear smuggled-in makeup. I'd have to walk around holding some tattooed skinhead's pocket.

I rubbed the caked sweat and vomit and pee and shit from my skin with soap. I dropped the soap many times because my hands hardly worked anymore. They were beyond shaking. I couldn't even fully open them to make a high-five. I dropped the soap again, trying to pick it up. This is how it will be. I'll drop the soap, as the saying goes, then get fucked in the ass. They'll take turns on a little bitch like me.

I was so scared, I puked. Yellowish water and nothing more. No food. I was starving. Truly starving.

The bathtub *crinked* and sunk more. I gave up on the soap and just got out. I certainly wasn't fully bathed, but it was better than before. Wrapped in an old towel, gaunt from throwing up so damn much.

I passed Gerald in the hallway and his oblivious ass said, "All set for me to go?"

I nodded and closed the bedroom door behind me.

Ma had stripped the bed of my disgusting piss-and-sweat-soaked sheets. I took a spare blanket from the closet, lay down on the bare mattress, and wallowed in extreme terror.

Nora had texted me saying, *Do you know where Frank is?*

They'd probably already caught him. I didn't have the will to respond to her. I was soon to be a ghost just like him.

It felt like it was never going to end. Every fissure of dread within me broke. It electrocuted my veins. It felt like it was never going to end.

Gerald was whistling in the shower.

And then they were at the door. The hogs. The detectives. Maybe even the fuckin' FBI. It was a homicide, after all.

I heard the powerful knocking at the front door, and then Ma saying, "Bobby, you need to come down here."

I found dusty pajamas and put them on. They were mismatched and a bit too snug. That's all I could find. These hogs with their fine-tailored suits and clean haircuts were about to come across this crazed, dope sick maniac with a weird fashion sense. There was no point in telling myself to just act natural. That was certainly out of the question.

Surprisingly, though, I felt a little bit better. I don't know if it was a shot of adrenaline or if I was just finally defeated. An escaped cow, now caught, about to be brought to the slaughterhouse. I don't know. The fear would return, though. I was sure of that.

Gerald was still whistling in the shower, so fuckin' clueless to all of this. I breathed deeply and made my way down.

I saw Ma sitting at the kitchen table, her face so worried. She looked at me then looked in front of her. But it wasn't the detectives who were in front of her. No.

It was Leslie, standing with my shotgun in her hands. "You weren't at your apartment, but I found this instead," she said through a chaw smile. "Sit down." She pointed the barrel at me, then a vacant chair.

Yep, now the fear was back.

Right in front of Leslie, on the table, was Catherine the cockatiel, dead. Leslie snapped her poor neck. A few feathers ripped out of her little, silent body.

I sat down slowly and watched the barrels of the shotgun follow me.

She smiled, then said, "Where?"

I said, "Where what?"

Of course, I knew who she meant. But now this was tricky because I truly didn't know where Frank was, but if I told her that, she'd just think I was covering for him. Loyalty and whatnot. If I gave him up too quickly, though, she might call the bluff.

"He's hiding," I said. "Hasn't told me shit."

Leslie shook her head, spit some mud out onto our floor.

I pulled this out of my ass and said, "He's got family down in New York City. But he'll be back. He will finish the job, just you wait."

"That's not gonna work for me, Bobby."

Something about her saying my name scared me. It was intimate. She knew me and I knew her.

Ma was sitting there with her hands up and close to her chest.

"Look," I said. "Ma's got nothing to do with this. Let her go."

"No," said Leslie.

"She's got *nothing* to do with it," I said.

Leslie gritted her teeth, making a bit of her chew chunk come loose. "You know what the funny thing is, Bobby? She does. She has a lot to do with it. She was the one who brought you into this world. If this white trash bitch didn't let you slither out of her snatch, I wouldn't have these problems."

"Fuck you, lady," said Ma.

Leslie hit Ma with the barrels.

Ma yelped.

Leslie smiled, then brought the gun back to me. She was all like, "You've got two minutes to talk or a slug for each of you."

I couldn't speak. This was how it was going to end. Gerald would hear the gunfire and find me and Ma lying dead on the floor. Our tongues hanging out, puddles of blood beneath us. This was it. Ma was about to die, because of me.

"Call him. Call his skank. Call his parents. Find out where he is, or I kill her first."

Well, I knew the skank she was referring to didn't know his whereabouts. I doubted he told his parents. And I doubted he was gonna answer my phone call. Basically, I knew I was fucked.

I said, "He's not gonna answer."

"Bobby, do it," said Ma.

How could I have done this? I wondered if I pounced on Leslie if that would give Ma enough time to escape. Maybe take my gun back into my arms and shoot her myself. A braver man would've done that. But instead, I took out my phone and called Frank.

I put it on speaker and placed the phone on the table. The light from the screen reflected in Catherine's open, dead eyes.

It rang, and we waited.

It rang.

It rang.

"The inbox of the person you're trying to reach is full..."

She was gonna do it. She was gonna kill us.

Leslie spat another wad. "One minute. Call the others."

I could've dialed Nora, but I was too afraid to move anymore. Leslie placed the barrels right to my forehead. Ma was weeping now. Seeing her one and only child moments from death. This would've been the snuff film of the decade if she was recording this. It'll be on the dark web, somewhere mixed in with the flayed man and all the Xanax and guns and other things Frank, Walter, and I took for granted. I could see into Leslie's eyes. Her head was positioned weird against the stock. Like she had never shot a gun before in her life. You'd think her eyes would look somewhat unnatural. A psychopath's eyes. Void of love. But no. They looked like anyone else's.

The ceiling started making a noise. A deep, crumbling noise. We all looked up. Water started cascading right through the drywall and paint. Then, came the screams of Gerald, and the bathtub crashed through the ceiling. Ma and I fell backward in our chairs and the tub landed right on top of Leslie. Gerald's naked body flopped down with it, like some huge and horrifying fish.

Gallons of water dumped over the table and floor, washing Catherine and the dip spit away. The bathtub broke into a bunch of porcelain pieces. I finally acted. The gun was unharmed and unfired on the floor, so I snagged it and pointed it at Leslie. Blood pumping through my sickly body, ready to kill.

But there was no need. She lay there, a great lesion on her head leaking blood onto the watery floor. Her eyes were open, too.

Gerald stood up and covered his wiener with his hands, all like, "Oh my God! Oh my God!"

It felt surreal, but Ma hugged me.

IV.

She actually didn't die—Leslie. But it made her a vegetable. She could do nothing but stare into open space, occasionally blinking. I wondered if she thought she did indeed shoot me before it all came tumbling down. I wondered if she still craved the sharp tobacco against her gums. The hogs would've got her, too, but that damn tub did the hard work for them.

It was a bizarre story, but like I said, A-Rod's killing was a walk in the park for them. They knew Frank did it and they knew I was there. They said they knew I was a good kid. Said I wasn't a bad man like my father was. Trying to make it seem like they were helping me. Typical hog shit, trying to appeal to my emotions. I wasn't expecting them to say that for all this to get better, I'd have to testify against Frank in a plea bargain. I had to snitch.

Every brand of criminal from the Yakuza to the Outlaws of the Ozarks hates a snitch. They're the lowest of the low in the criminal world. Biker Gangs? My dad? Do you know what they'd do to snitches? They wouldn't just kill them. No, no. That's too quick. They'd poke their eyeballs out with shanks. They'd jump them in the kitchen and shove their head in the oven. There is nothing worse than a snitch, but I did it. I told the hogs everything.

♦♦♦

It took time but they managed to track Frank down. They found him in a motel room on the outskirts of Columbus, Ohio. He had a stash of crank with him. Probably tweaking and got into a scuffle with them.

It was awkward seeing Frank in the courtroom. He didn't look any different. Even me, his clear ride-or-die, wasn't given even a single look of, *I'll kill you in the mess hall.* Maybe he felt the guilt now even though I stabbed him in the back. He got life, of course. You'd think he might've flinched when the judge said that. You'd think he might've put his head down. I don't know. Anything. Any sort of reaction would've done. But there was nothing. He remained utterly emotionless, even with his mom sobbing like crazy. That was the first time I'd seen her show emotion.

We got put in different joints. I was off to Attica. I got seven, plus crazy probation after. Middling conspiracy charges and they threw assault in with it. The public defender didn't do much for me. Should've known by his baggy suit. How poetic.

Like Ma once told me, gotta have a backup plan. Walter's freak-ass was the most loyal of us all. I gave him instructions to burn all the remaining drugs and the laptop. Gave him the coordinates so he could dig up the drug cash, too. My first letter from Ma confirmed he got it all to her. Said she bought some wacky Gucci purse. Some things never change. Guess Ma could experience the so-called "high life" she always wanted. Maybe get another bird or a whole flock of them.

♦♦♦

Prison is boring as shit, as you can imagine. The meals are just small enough where you don't feel satisfied, but you get used to it, eventually. They have A.A. here, and it's been helping me. I got through it, but I think my brain is fried for the long run. Burns and cuts and bruises are all just mini trophies of all my fuck ups. I still don't feel normal.

Fortunately, reading and writing is a hobby you can support

behind bars. It's all I really have time to do. My dad gave me some pointers. And with that, I was able to write full drafts of something. The very story I'm telling you, of course. It took a shit load of time. Hell, I couldn't even write the first year since I was still scared shitless.

♦♦♦

I was standing out in the yard with my dad, and he asked, "What's new on the outside world? I've been locked away for years now."

"Well," I said. "People's cell phones are now phones, computers, cameras, and TVs all in one."

"I already knew that," he said. "Everyone talks about that. What's something that I wouldn't expect if I got out?"

It was hard to think of something on the spot.

"A lot of girls have been getting this pierced." I pinched my septum with two fingers.

"What now?" he said.

"Yeah," I said.

"Like a bull?"

"Like a bull."

"What the hell?"

"It's kind of cute on the right type of girl. I don't know."

"Fuck that."

"Better than a mullet, from your generation."

"You know what Bobby," he said, "you might be right about that."

The two of us stood there with our hands at our sides. We watched the inmates come and go. Nearly all of them looked older than they really were. They were strong and tattooed and seldom smiled. They were mindful of eye contact. They were alert. You'd think in a place where there was little to do but be languid, the inmates would be more languid. No. We were on edge.

Territorial, these men. Each race, each gang, each clique, had their section of the yard to converse and you stayed within your border unless you wanted trouble.

It was good to have my dad there. The whites weren't all biker outlaws as he was, but they accepted him, and thus, they accepted me. In that way, this birthright was misinterpreted as a privilege.

I didn't look at my dad, just said, "You can say I told you so."

He waited for a moment as if he didn't hear me.

"That would do no good," he finally said.

"Are you mad at me?"

"No, I'm mad at myself."

Now I was silent for a moment. I was wearing the same pathetic slippers as him. I rubbed them against the concrete. "It's not your fault," I told him.

"It is," he said. He looked at me. "You're not in here forever. You've still got your whole life ahead of you when you get out."

"Yeah, like I'll be able to get a job as a felon."

"Quit bitching. At least you'll have your freedom. I'd rather live in a tent and pick food out of dumpsters than live in here." He was glaring at me, then his head shot back to center. He exhaled, closed his eyes, and brought his hand to his face. He brought it back down and opened his eyes again. "I'm sorry," he said. "You'll figure it out. I know you will. They've got programs for felons."

Burly white men with long beards and bald heads and biceps bigger than my thighs lifted weights before us. Their teeth were bad. Their skin was bad. Some of them had faces that just looked wrong, as if God wanted them to be sinners, and molded their faces so.

"How do you live with it?" I asked.

"Live with what?"

I didn't answer.

"Oh," he said. "I don't. It hardly feels like I'm alive anymore."

I wanted to cry, but there was no crying in this place.

An elder hobbled by and looked at us. He was short and crooked. His eyes weren't what they used to be. He stopped.

"Father and son?" he asked.

"Yeah."

"I can tell."

He stayed looking for a moment, like some ancient theologian staring at some blurry visage in some unexpected holy light. Or something like that. I don't know.

About the Author

Joseph Sigurdson is a writer and poet from Buffalo, New York. He's the recipient of the Edwin Markham Award and the winner of the Gabriele Rico Challenge for Nonfiction from *Reed Magazine*. His work has appeared in *The Buffalo News, South 85, Columbia Journal,* and elsewhere. His first chapbook of prose poetry, *No Sand*, was published by Thirty West Publishing in 2019. *Buffalo Dope* is his first novel.

Thirty West Publishing House

Handmade chapbooks (and more) since 2015

Follow us on Instagram, Twitter, & Facebook:

@thirtywestph

thirtywestph.com